PICK IT UP!

BECCA SPENCE DOBIAS

ABOVE THE TREE HOUSE

***

To Jer, who is better than a fantasy.
To my family and former teachers—please skip chapters 11 and 24.

CHAPTER 1: SAILOR

There was no faux turkey left in the vegetarian aisle at the health food store.

"I'll look in the specials freezer in the back." Roger motioned past the aisles of bulk grains. "You go ask someone."

"No, you ask, and I'll look." I picked up a box of almond flour crackers and scanned the ingredients, trying to avoid my friend's eyes.

"Sailor, you are a grown ass woman. You don't have to be afraid of strangers anymore."

"I'm not afraid." I huffed and put down the crackers. "I just don't like talking to them."

With a roll of his eyes, Roger turned to walk to the front of the store, which was bustling with other last-minute shoppers.

"You love me," I called after him.

"You're lucky I do," he called back, and I could hear the smile in his voice.

The freezer in the back was almost empty, too, but I moved aside boxes of organic pumpkin pies and hormone free chicken nuggets, hoping to find some buried soy. Roger returned a minute later.

"The extremely cute employee said vegan turkey sells out two weeks before every major holiday."

"Did you at least get his number?" I let the cauliflower crust pizza I was holding fall back into the freezer.

"He was very cute *and* very straight."

I groaned and grabbed the sleeve of Roger's blazer to drag him back to the car. "I guess it's green beans and tabouli salad for Thanksgiving. It would have been nice if my mom had asked us to bring a protein before today. I should have known she'd flake on it."

We'd parked in the sun, and despite it being November, the inside of the car was dense with heat. My phone dinged as I buckled my seatbelt. I adjusted the strap between my boobs and checked the message.

"Shit."

"Another one?" Roger asked.

"Yuuuuup." I scrubbed my hand down my face. I'd lost three drum students in the past month.

"Who this time?"

"Diya."

"No!" Roger looked genuinely pained. "Not Diya. We loved Diya. I'm sorry." Roger had never met Diya, or any of my students save for the ones he taught himself, but he listened attentively to all my stories, rolling his eyes at all the right parts and clutching his heart at every sweet moment I shared.

I closed my eyes and sighed. "I don't know how I'm going to pay you for rent this month."

Behind us, a car honked, waiting for the spot. I took a deep breath and tried to pull myself together. "Let's go."

"They can wait," Roger said.

My best friend understood me like no one else could. He and the music had been the only constants in my life. With a mom like mine, full of love and wisdom but decidedly short on structure and stability, I had clung to both of them. Ska gave me an ideology, an identity, when my mom flitted from obsession to obsession, be it Kabbalah or I-ching. And Roger had given me security—not only financial, but emotional. He was sturdy, and he didn't let me take any shit, even from myself.

The former trumpet player in our high school band, the Skankin' Kiddos, Roger was the only bandmate I was still in touch with. There had been a few awkward group texts and emails after graduation—a few half-hearted comments about really needing to find a time to play again, but of course the time never came. No one, aside from me and Roger, had cared about the band like we did, and eventually I'd understood my hope for a revival was a delusion. So the two of us had rearranged our dreams—found different ways to keep music central to our lives, and stuck together. His strategy was more successful than mine.

Roger had toned down his look since our Skankin' Kiddos days, and I got it. He was already the gay, Black music teacher at the conservative private school; he didn't need to give parents further reason to be wary of his influence. But Roger was still Roger—my best friend for over a decade now, and my recurring savior when it came to finances.

Now, he patted my arm lovingly.

I opened my eyes. "I guess I can ask to take on more shifts at the diner, but..."

"Shush. Don't worry about it right now." Roger squeezed my arm and tipped his head forward to make sure I was looking him in the eye. "You'll just have to do more dishes to earn your keep. Besides, when you get your big break, you'll pay me back easily." Behind the joke, I could hear the worry in his voice. I'd been hemorrhaging students, and teacher salaries were not known for being great. Roger was easily stressed out, and he'd seemed even more on edge lately. I hated adding to his burden. As much as I appreciated his generosity, we both knew there was no break coming. With every passing day, drawing us further and further from the ska boom of the early 2000s, the demand for my drum skills diminished—my dreams along with it. But I was stubborn. I'd thrown too much away to give them up now.

"Thank you," I said.

"Don't mention it. Now let's go."

At Rainbow's, a mossy Buddha statue greeted us at the door, and several pots over-flowing with hanging succulents hung from the wooden patio cover. We entered without knocking and found my mother sitting at the kitchen table studying a tarot spread.

"Your house doesn't change," I said. As fickle as my mom could be, her decor, at least, was consistent.

Rainbow turned and smiled. "Don't be silly." She stood. "I've acquired some new crystals for my shelves."

"And some new succulents," I said. "I told you to stop stealing plants from your neighbors."

"And I've told *you* it isn't stealing. They won't miss one cutting, especially when I use it to propagate even more beauty for the neighborhood."

She turned her gaze to Roger, took in his slim mohair suit, porkpie hat, and shiny loafers, and put a hand to her heart. "Oh, darling! You look so handsome in your nasty boy outfit."

"Mom!" I said, momentarily forgetting her chosen name in my embarrassment. "It's 'rude boy.' Jesus." Surely I had mentioned the signature ska style dozens of times, but Roger cackled.

"Rainbow, you can call me a nasty boy any time you want." He took my mother into his arms and kissed her frizzy brown hair.

I was next, and as I hugged Rainbow's wispy frame, I took in her signature patchouli and weed scent before my awareness settled on the splotchy glass of the windows over her shoulder. "I'll call Mariska and tell her you need another deep clean." I pulled away to examine the windows more closely. Sure enough, the sills were covered in grime, the less appealing manifestation of the incense ash and marijuana smoke of her personal smell.

Rainbow ignored me. "Look. I have a new book for the coffee table. It's about chakras! And a new tarot deck. I haven't had a chance to charge it yet, but I was looking it over before you arrived and I think it will be wonderfully intuitive."

"Mm," I muttered, thankful we wouldn't be subjected to tarot readings tonight.

I'd gotten dinner partially correct. Rainbow did, indeed, set out a tabouli salad full of cherry tomatoes, sliced cucumber, and mint from her herb garden. Instead of green beans, though, the other colorful ceramic serving dishes were filled with sliced avocado, roasted Brussel sprouts, crispy chickpeas, and sautéed spinach and garlic. My mom might have been absentminded sometimes, but I didn't give her enough credit for her cooking skills.

"I'm thankful for my beautiful daughter and her beautiful roommate." Rainbow looked at me as she took a slow, savoring breath. "And for the cosmos bringing us to this moment, together."

"I'm thankful for wine," I said, as I poured myself a glass.

Roger laughed. "I'm thankful to be sitting between two gorgeous women...and for wine." We all laughed now, and I filled Roger's glass next. The three of us ate in contented silence for several minutes, the faux turkey unmissed.

Rainbow finished first, setting her silverware neatly beside her plate. "Sailor, can you take a look at my dryer when you have a chance? It hasn't been drying as efficiently the last week or so. If it were summer, I would set up the line, but with the Santa Anas, I think my clothes might end up dirtier than before if I hung them out. I hate wasting energy but it's been taking two or three rounds to get them even partially dry."

"Have you been cleaning out the lint trap like I showed you?" I asked through a bite of spinach.

"Mmm! That's it!" Rainbow threw a finger in the air like an old time scientist discovering a new principle. "Can you show me where it is again? When you're done with dinner. Thank you, love."

My mom was going to burn the house down.

After a refresher course on dryer anatomy and a dessert of butternut squash pie, I leaned back in my chair and put my hands on my belly, sleepy and satiated. "Everything was delicious. Thank you."

"Delectable as always," Roger chimed in.

Rainbow beamed. "You two should visit more often."

I was too full to point out how I was already at my mom's house at least once a week to help her with various tasks—changing the air conditioning filter or snaking hair from the shower drain.

"Shall we gather as usual for the last night of Hannukah?" Rainbow asked.

"Sure." I eyed what was left of the pie and wondered if I could squeeze in another slice.

"Actually." Roger's voice was quieter than usual, lacking its usual jubilance.

My gaze snapped to him. Actually what? Roger was obsessed with my mom. Everything I found annoying—her inability to blend in, her colorful patchwork skirts, her essential oils and oracle cards—he found endearing, and he'd told me once he wanted to be her when he grew up. Unlike other people who knew Rainbow, Roger understood why she could be difficult, and I always knew his loyalty lay with me, but still, he adored her. And Jewish holidays were probably next on Roger's list of favorite things. He loved our yearly nontraditional Hannukah tradition, with its sweet potato pancakes and homemade carob gelt.

"What?" I prodded.

Roger fiddled with his tie, glancing from me to Rainbow. He looked nervous. Finally, he spit it out. "I can't do the last night of Hannukah."

My confusion evaporated and my heart dropped. I knew, suddenly, what he was going to say next. His recent anxiety. The increased flightiness.

"I'm moving back to New York. That's the day I leave."

Anticipating the words didn't lessen their impact, and my head spun—the wine hitting the same moment as the statement. I'd been fearing this moment since the day things ended between me and Jake over a decade earlier—when Roger became my only lifeline in a place I never felt I belonged. He'd promised me he'd be here. I knew he hadn't meant forever, but I needed him. Didn't he know how much I needed him? I blinked, trying to still my swimming vision. I gripped the table and realized my hands were shaking.

"Wonderful!" Rainbow said, her brightness grating. "What will you be doing there?"

"Leading a boys' choir in the city."

Despite his attempts to appear cool, there were tears in the corner of my best friend's eyes.

I took a deep breath, attempting again to regain control of my nervous system. Roger and Rainbow both walked on eggshells around my temper sometimes, and I was determined not to let the focus shift to me. I needed to stay calm—maybe this was fixable.

"I thought you loved your job." It was all I could think of to say, and I knew it was a pathetic bid. Of course teaching middle school music couldn't compare to leading a boy's choir. It was a dream gig and a chance for his New Yorker heart to escape bad pizza and bagels, fake niceness, and car dependency. This was so perfect for Roger, and I wanted so badly to be happy for him.

"I do love my job, but honey," Roger's eyes looked sad. "It's not enough anymore."

"Oh." My own tears threatened and I blinked them away. *I* was not enough anymore. In spite of the rationalizing I'd done a moment ago, I was suddenly certain of what he meant. Again, I was not enough to make someone stay.

"I'm so sorry." He swallowed and glanced quickly at Rainbow.

He knew this had been the wrong place to bring this up, but when exactly had he planned to tell me?

"And you know my family has really come around. Their new church is very accepting. They've done the work, and I feel like I need to meet them halfway now. They're my blood, and I miss them, and they're trying."

This stung too. Roger was my family, blood or not.

"Finally!" Rainbow gave Roger's hand a squeeze, then looked me in the eye. "I know this must be hard for you, sweetheart, emotionally and financially. You know you are always welcome to move back into your old room."

A cold, hard fear stabbed through me. I hadn't even considered the house. There was no way I could pay for rent alone. And there was no way I could move back in with my mom. The kitchen instantly felt smaller as I pictured eating breakfast here each morning, Rainbow commenting on my aura or whatever new age thing she got into next. I knew I needed to be nearby for her, but not *so* nearby.

Suddenly, I remembered Roger comforting me in the car, the slight hesitance I'd sensed in his reassurances. He had known he was leaving. Is this what he had meant when he'd told me not to worry about rent—that I could move back in with Rainbow?

I stood up from my chair, my full stomach now uncomfortable rather than pleasant. "I need to go." I turned toward the front door. Roger's chair scraped the floor behind me as he stood to follow.

"Sorry," he apologized to my mom. "Thank you. Dinner was perfect."

I felt dazed on the ride home, removed from my own reality, unable to think clearly about what was happening or what it meant. Roger was silent, not even moving to turn on music. I wanted to be in my room, under my covers. When we arrived home a minute later, I stumbled in the door and got into bed, still reeling, and opened the music app on my phone. The posters on my walls peered down from the dark.

A moment later, Roger knocked quietly.

"Do you want to talk about it?" he asked from the other side of the door.

"Not right now." I sensed his pause, then listened as his footsteps retreated down the hall.

Diya had insisted on learning One Direction at her last lesson, and the band was still on my Recently Played. I clicked over to my favorites, but as I saw my usual artists appear, I knew what I needed to listen to. It was Thanksgiving—almost time for the winter holidays. It was time for *Happy Skalidays*.

Silently, I thanked Roger for refusing to let Jake ruin the album for me—for ensuring I associated the music not only with my first boyfriend and the band his decisions had torn apart, but with my best friend, too.

The part of me that did think about Jake when I heard it hurt a little less each year. Last year's listen had left me almost wistful as I remembered the feeling of my leg touching Jake's, of looking at his grin, of kissing him on the couch.

Our time together had been nice. I missed it, even, and this was a way to bring it back. With a pang, I realized Roger would be a painful association now too, but I would take a play from his book—I wouldn't let him ruin the music for me either. In time, I would be able to hear the songs and think back to our time as roommates fondly, but I would have to rip the bandage off and shoulder the sickly sweet pain of listening to it first.

I typed the album name into the search bar. I would always have music, I told myself. Music would never leave me.

As I waited for the results to load, I could already picture the first song and hear the opening notes, but where the album usually appeared, I saw... nothing. Or nothing relevant, anyway.

There were the spell-corrected "Happy Holidays" playlists, "Oi to the World" by the Vandals and the cover by No Doubt, which I hated to admit was really fucking good. Someone had hashtagged "Happy Skalidays" in the description. There was a user-made playlist called Skalidays which contained not ska but songs by Social Distortion with their signature skeleton mascot.

I scrolled and scrolled, but the results got less and less relevant. There were no video results either—nothing even close.

My urge to self-soothe began to devolve into further frustration, and I cursed myself, as I had so many times, for my fantastic blow-up in high school. If I hadn't stormed out of the venue in such a rage, I could have gotten physical copies of all of Agents of Ska's albums. They may have even *given* me copies of their albums.

Inspired by my self-flagellation, I searched for used copies. Their other albums came up immediately, though they were listed for outrageous prices—someone wanted $799 for a mint condition copy of their white vinyl debut—but seeing them exist somewhere was reassuring.

Again, I scrolled and scrolled, ignoring my visceral reaction to the old familiar images— neon backgrounds with the band members in various poses, decked out as their secret agent alter egos, the album titles in blocky comic book font.

But in seven pages of results, there was not a single copy of *Happy Skalidays*, even when I ensured I didn't have filters selected for price, condition, or anything else. *Hm.*

Hearing a sound in my doorway, I looked up to find Desmond, Roger's eight-year-old French Bulldog, her white fur short and neat, her little face wrinkled with concern.

"It's ok, Des," I said.

The pup wagged her tail stub and came to sit by my bed, then settled into a furry cinnamon bun heap as I resumed my search.

I checked the band's own website next, but this apparently no longer existed. Even the archive seemed lost to the far reaches of the Internet past. What the fuck? How could an album just...disappear?

"Where'd it go Des?" I rolled onto my side and looked down at Roger's dog. Tongue hanging from her mouth, she let out a comically long snore.

I knew all too well people could vanish from your life, but music…music was supposed to be my touchstone. Losing an album was like losing a part of myself. I needed desperately to find it.

APRIL 18, 2013

xDrummerChickx: Hey Roger. Thanks for coming with me after the show. I didn't need your pity though. Even if I did freak.

GaYrUdEbOySUnItE: Girl, I didn't pity you. I just needed a ride home. Still mad you wouldn't let us listen to Agents of Ska though. You always listen to a band on the way back after their show

xDrummerChickx: I didn't want to associate them with bad feelings :(

GaYrUdEbOySUnItE: that's why you listen as much as possible. Don't give him that power. It's m-fing Agents of Ska! He doesn't own them!

xDrummerChickx: maybe you're right.

GaYrUdEbOySUnItE: I know I am! Go listen now and think about me instead…you know you're too cool for him right?

xDrummerChickx: I did introduce him to ska

GaYrUdEbOySUnItE: see?? He was a dork before you

xDrummerChickx: he's still a dork but I love him

GaYrUdEbOySUnItE: well you love me too and I'm not going anywhere anytime soon

xDrummerChickx: I'm glad

★ ★ ★ ★ ★ ★

CHAPTER 2: JAKE

I t was too long a drive for people who had nothing real to say to each other. Bored and unable to look at my phone, my mind reached for distraction, landing on the comedy special I'd watched last night after Hillary had gone to sleep.

"What' so funny?" Hillary asked.

I startled. I hadn't realized I was smirking.

"Nothing." She wouldn't appreciate the joke about ball sacks.

Hillary went back to filling the silence with work drama, and I went back to responding in various "mmms."

The good "mmms" were shorter, a little upturned at the end, a head tilt for good measure. The bad ones were deeper and longer, with a serious lowering of the eyebrows.

The principal was trying to cut funds to her program again (mmmmmm), but she had a new plan to get all the choir parents involved in a letter writing campaign (mmm!).

"We'll back it up with a prayer circle, of course." Hillary lowered her voice conspiratorially. "The Christian part will have to stay unofficial so Roger won't complain, though if it comes down to it, I'm sure I can drag up some dirt. And if it persuades Fletcher to divert some of his budget my way..." she smiled. "Then I guess our prayer will have worked."

My brow furrowed in earnest. "That's fucked, Hill."

Her head snapped to me. "Language!"

We were both surprised at my actual commentary, but her plan to throw our former bandmate under the bus had caught me off guard. Still, I knew it wasn't worth getting into. Hillary's morals were strictly God-related.

By the time we turned into Hillary's parents' Sacramento neighborhood, I had gone fully dissociative, and when we pulled up to their towering McMansion, the thought occurred to me, not for the first time, that I'd been suckered into a plan she'd had for me all along—a plan she was both proud she had pulled off and disappointed she couldn't make fit her exact specifications. She'd gotten me, but she hadn't quite been able to mold me the way she'd hoped. I was a constant disappointment.

At some point during our sophomore year of college, Hillary had convinced me to let my guard down by showing me her silly side. She could be goofy and fun, even if her idea of fun was the wholesome camp games we'd played at the Christian Student Alliance meetings she'd dragged me to when I visited her at Stanford.

The people there wanted me to change, too. Behind their hugs was the hope they could recruit me—that by being extra nice, they might bring me to Jesus. They didn't care about me. They wanted brownie points with their savior.

But Hillary's love had felt different. She wanted me to go to church with her, too, but it was because she wanted us to go to Heaven together. It was another sticking point—something we'd fought and cried about over and over, until there was no point discussing it anymore—disappointment number one in a long line.

I told myself what I always did when these thoughts arose. Sailor and I had broken up for a reason. No matter the reason was because I, myself, had made the dumb decision to leave for Berkeley. I was shortsighted and immature, but Sailor had been, too. She'd been stuck in her high school fantasies and unsupportive of my ambitions, no matter how misguided my dreams may have been. Hillary was mature, ambitious in a realistic way, and unlike Sailor, she made compromises for our relationship. She tolerated her disappointment instead of lashing out.

"Are you ready?" Hillary asked, snapping me back to the present. She looked beautiful, despite the long drive, in a frilly green knee-length dress and sexy red lipstick. Her sleek blonde hair was swooshed into some kind of fancy twist. Her eyes sparkled.

"I am one hundred percent ready to crush some turkey." But as I moved to unbuckle my seatbelt, my phone rang from the center console. We looked at the screen, "Ma" scrolling across it. "In one minute."

Annoyance flashed behind Hillary's sparkle but she didn't say a word.

"You look pretty," I said, and her smile returned. "What are you? A flower? Get out of here with that grin." Hillary blushed and tipped her head toward my phone, motioning for me to answer.

"Hi, sweetheart," my mom said when I picked up. "Did you forget about your mother on Thanksgiving?"

"Of course not, Ma. I would never forget about you. I was going to call tonight. We're about to go in to the Decklands'."

"I ordered my noodles. From Shanghai Bistro, not from Wok In. You know I told you last time Wok In gave me terrible constipation."

The older my mother got, the more I had to hear about the state of her bowels.

Beside me, Hillary wrinkled her nose and furrowed her brow. My mom was loud enough Hillary had to hear it too. In all the time we'd been together, I had heard her fart exactly once—the cutest little squeak—after which, she'd turned bright red and dashed to the bathroom. At home, Hillary kept a bottle of rose scented spray on a shelf above the toilet and streamed worship music on her phone whenever she went.

I lowered my voice. "I know, Ma."

"I bought more prune juice at the store today, but still. You know I hate being constipated."

"Yep, I know. Anyone asks me what my mom hates the most, I tell them it's constipation." I smiled at Hillary apologetically.

"Oh! You know who I ran into at the store when I was getting the juice? You'll never believe it."

"Who, Ma?" In the seat beside me, Hillary raised her eyebrows, signaling me to wrap it up, and I felt torn between wanting my mom to talk longer, postponing our entrance, and wanting the call to end so my girlfriend didn't get angry. I held up a finger to Hillary and nodded. She sighed.

"Rainbow Grinspoon! Do you remember her?"

For a moment I was too stunned to respond. I thought about Sailor way more than I wanted to admit, and the invocation of her mother made me feel like a thirteen year old with a boner, like every one of my fantasies was on full display.

"You and her daughter Sailor were in the band."

"Oh really? I'd forgotten," I deadpanned.

My mom went on. "And then you were special friends for awhile. Such strange names, but I really liked them. I almost thought you two might get married one day." I glanced at Hillary to see if she was still listening and found she'd retreated into her own phone. I knew she was waiting for me to finish up the call. She didn't trust me to make a decent entrance on my own.

"I know, Ma." She had told me every day for a month after Sailor and I broke up how she'd been so happy I'd found a nice Jewish girl and how she was so sad it hadn't worked out, and how you never knew—maybe we'd come back to each other someday.

"Anyway, she told me Sailor's roommate is leaving—the nice African American boy who stayed with us for a while, always so polite that one."

I cringed at my mother's subtle racism.

"He's going back to New York. I guess there are probably more homosexuals there so he'll feel more at home."

Now I cringed at the homophobia. My mom really was on the right side of most issues, but you wouldn't know it from her language. Her voice trailed off. "Anyway, darling. I'd better let you go to your party."

"Um...yeah," I stuttered. "Enjoy your noodles. Happy Thanksgiving."

"Oh, you know I will, dear. I just hope my stomach does."

"Me too, Ma. Keep me updated."

"Jacob Rosenblatt!" she scolded. I laughed, and reluctantly, she did too. We both hung up and I stared blankly at my phone, trying to absorb the information about Sailor. My mind was racing. Roger was leaving? Was he ok? Was Sailor ok? Was she still teaching drum lessons? Where would she live if Roger wasn't there?

Hillary looked up from her phone. "Done?"

"Why didn't you mention Roger's leaving?" Their classrooms were adjacent—surely she knew.

Hillary shrugged. "Didn't you enjoy assuming I'm a monster for wanting his funding? I wouldn't want to take that away from you."

"Oh, no," I said in a mock-serious tone. "The demonic ramblings in your sleep are what made me assume you're a monster. And those vials of blood you keep behind the fizzy water."

But I knew why Hillary hadn't told me. She hadn't wanted me to think about Sailor and her living situation. Like ska, Roger moving would be a reminder of something unpleasant—something Hillary categorized alongside regrettable high school fashion choices and outdated tech.

"All the more reason why Roger shouldn't have a say in the department's programming," she said, ignoring my joke. "Why should I have to adjust my budget when they can take the money from whoever comes in to replace him?"

Without waiting for my response, she swung open her door and stepped out into the chilly evening.

"Jesus, it's friggin' cold up here," I said, as I opened my door to join her.

Outside the car, Hillary looked me up and down, and I shook my arms and head like I was about to go onstage—it was performance time.

As Hillary picked lint from my shirt, I lifted my chin to take in the whole of her parents' house. Above the three-car garage, its expansive beige facade was punctuated by white-trimmed windows, as boring as the cookie cutter houses in SoCal. Why had the Decklands bothered to move? Sacramento was basically the Inland Empire, the region we'd grown up in, but even more boring and with worse weather. For a split second, I considered how I could spin this to encourage my own mom to move North—close enough to see her for holidays, but not so close I felt responsible for staving off her loneliness. God, I was a shitty son.

"You look handsome," Hillary said.

I pulled myself from my musings and smiled at the unexpected compliment.

"Well thank you, kind miss." I put one hand across my stomach, imitating a butler. When was the last time Hillary had complimented me? Maybe the stress of work had gotten to us both. Maybe all we needed was a little fresh air and some no-pressure time together.

"Have you thought any more about teeth aligners?" My body went hot as my gut tightened. Snapping my lips closed, I smoothed my button down shirt, sucking in my belly so it didn't hang over my nice khaki pants quite as much. Hillary had been eyeing it with controlled disdain lately. One night after I'd gone to bed, she'd sent me, without comment, an article about how obesity in parents was more likely to lead to conceiving a boy. Apparently Hillary wanted to have girls.

Inside, the party was what I'd expected—cousins and aunts and uncles and grandparents all dressed up, everyone hugging Hillary and saying "Happy Thanksgiving," then giving me polite nods.

Alan Deckland, Hillary's father, pulled his daughter to his chest and scowled over her shoulder at me.

"Jacob. How are you?"

"I'm good, man. How's it going?"

"Let's sit," Belinda Deckland cut in. She slipped a stick-like arm between Alan and Hillary, and guided them both toward the table. I followed behind like a scraggly shelter pet adopted on a whim, only allowed to stay because rehoming me would tarnish their warm, welcoming image.

Dinner, too, was the same as every year--delicious and too-filling, no alcohol in sight, the conversation an hour of extended small talk.

"Have you watched any new shows lately?" someone asked.

"I started a new sitcom but the language is a bit excessive."

I contributed several "mmmms" as I ate, and feigned agreement by occasionally pointing my fork at a speaker as they went on.

"Good potatoes, Belinda."

"They are! Did you use a new recipe?"

"Oh, no. Same old recipe."

"Well, they're scrumptious."

Suddenly, Alan Deckland turned straight to me. "How long have you two been together now?" He pointed his chin toward his daughter.

Of course, I had just taken a bite of turkey. The whole table stared as I chewed for a very long minute.

I swallowed with a gulp, feeling every millimeter of dry meat as it slid down my throat. "About nine years now, right Hill?" I looked at Hillary, desperate to divert the attention.

"Yeah, it was nine in August. The first week of sophomore year."

Alan kept his eyes on me as he tipped his head to his wife. Everyone else feigned interest in their food. "How long did I court you before we got engaged?"

Hillary's mother pretended to think. "Six months or so."

"Mm." Alan nodded slowly.

I didn't have to let this man intimidate me. I schooled my face into a smile and took another bite of turkey. "Times sure are 'a changin," I said, mouth full.

But Alan didn't bite. "What was the article you sent me, Hillary, sweetheart? About fertility after 30? And how that IVF nonsense is a sin?"

I didn't even try to suppress my eye roll as I swallowed.

"Yeah, it said most people who do IVF end up with unused embryos that either stay frozen or get discarded."

I glared at my girlfriend, who at least had the decency to look sheepish. Fuck not fighting. We would be talking about this.

Belinda shook her head. "Poor babies." She actually looked like she might cry.

"They're not ba—" I cut myself off. It wasn't worth it. I wouldn't win that argument here. I took a sip of my sparkling water, trying to keep it together.

Alan set his fork down with a clatter. "You going to ask for my blessing soon, son?"

I coughed and spit a bit of my drink into the cloth napkin. I hadn't been expecting the directness. Recovering, I looked at my lap.

"Oy, well, you know, in Judaism, we usually ask for the father's curse. The goblin thing, you know. I'm not sure how it works in interfaith situations."

Alan turned away from me with unguarded contempt and shared a look with Belinda, who was still on the brink of tears. Maybe they would decide they'd rather their daughter stay unmarried than stay with a heathen.

Under the table, Hillary stomped on my foot with her heel, and I had to stifle my yelp. What the fuck was happening?

"What did you use for the cake this year, Susan?" Belinda asked, and the family turned their attention to one of Hillary's aunts.

Susan folded her hands on the table. "The same Betty Crocker white cake mix. It's so simple it should be a sin."

As they went on about the cake, I sat stunned, staring at my half-empty china plate.

The Decklands' conversations rarely had much substance at all, and yet, Hillary's father had put me on the spot out of nowhere.

My face growing hot, I excused myself to go to the restroom. There, I loosened my collar and splashed cold water on my face.

When I got back to the table, it was as if nothing had happened. The awkwardness had dissipated, and the conversation had shifted to the new secretary at the Decklands' church, who had spent double the budgeted amount on printer paper.

I ate the rest of my food in silence, barely tasting it, then sat and let my eyes glaze over as I waited for the Decklands to finish their meal, bites timed between the inane chatter.

"Cake?" Aunt Susan held a dish of spongy dessert under my nose. Its frosting smelled sticky and sweet.

"No thank you."

She set my portion before Hillary, and I waited again, as folks finished the sinfully simple confection.

At last, the final fork found its way back to the table.

"Are you done, Jake?" Hillary pointed to my dinner plate, avoiding eye contact.

I nodded. I was certainly starting to feel done.

Hillary and the other women began to clear the dishes. As usual, I moved to help, and as usual, the older women tsked until I gave up and retreated to the family room with the other men. There, I sat on the floral couch, taking up as little space as possible, wishing this was a Jewish holiday. What I would give for a glass of kosher wine or four.

The doorbell rang, but before anyone could answer, in tumbled more people—Hillary's very pregnant, very blonde cousin Vicky, and Vicky's very tall husband Brian, with his very Proud Boy mustache and haircut.

"Sorry, Uncle Alan." Vicky's stomach came to a point at her navel, like a tummy torpedo. "Brian's family dinner ran long."

Behind them was their daughter Sofie, her hair blonde too, with a puff of curls setting her apart. I could tell from the sofa she'd grown since I'd seen her at Easter. She wouldn't look at anyone.

"Come on, Sofie," her mother coaxed. "Come out and give everyone hugs."

Sofie stayed put, clinging to Vicky's legs. I could relate. Brian rolled his eyes. "We talked about this. You're going to be a big girl. Let go of Mommy."

"Heil. I mean hi, Brian," I said. "Hey, Vicky. What's good?"

Slowly, Sofie emerged, tears welling in her big blue eyes.

"Go on." Vicky patted her daughter between the shoulder blades.

A single tear rolled down Sofie's cheek, and something in me snapped. "You don't have to hug anyone if you don't want to." The words were out of my mouth before I could think them through, the confrontation at dinner hanging over me.

Ignoring me, Alan Deckland rose from his chair and went to shake Brian's hand.

"Aw, Sofie. Look at Poppy." Vicky squatted, her belly resting on her thighs. "You'd better hug him so you don't hurt his feelings." Alan twisted his face into a clownish frown.

Sofie began to shuffle toward Alan.

"I don't know if telling her to give people physical affection when she doesn't want to is the best precedent to set. Maybe we shouldn't think about other people's desires more than her own," I called from the couch.

Brian and Alan both glared at me.

"You do want her to be confident protecting her virginity, I assume." I hated myself for pulling this card, but it was probably the only way to get through to this crowd.

Alan cleared his throat. "Maybe the boy's got a point." Back straight, he moved from the entryway back toward the family room with Sofie and her parents following behind.

The little girl looked at me with something like awe before taking a deep breath, running to me, jumping onto my lap, and catching me in a tight embrace. "Will you play astronaut?" Sofie's voice was small and hopeful.

"Whoooooah, Astronaut?" I looked around in feigned astonishment. "How did you know? I friggin' love playing astronaut. Will I play astronaut?" I scoffed. "You aren't gonna be able to get me to *stop* playing astronaut."

"Yay!" Sofie tugged on my hand and pulled me up from the couch. Without another word to Alan or her parents, I let her lead me up to the play room on the second floor, with a shelf housing an old copy of Parcheesi, its box faded, and an equally-worn copy of the King James Bible.

"You're the bad alien and I'm the good astronaut and you're trying to blow up the world but I'm going to stop you," Sofie said.

"No fair. How come you get to be the good one?"

Sofie giggled.

"Just kidding." I let out an exaggerated evil laugh. "I love being the villain. Watch out, world. Evil Jake Alien is blowing you up today!" I began stumbling around the room in slow motion zero gravity mode, reaching for my invisible space cannon.

Sofie shrieked. "Not today, Evil Jake Alien! The Planet Protector is here!" She tackled me and I fell to the floor, both of us giggling.

Twenty minutes later, I was so engrossed in our game, I didn't notice Hillary standing in the doorway until she spoke. "Uncle Jake's fun, isn't he?"

We both turned, suddenly back to real life, and Sofie nodded. "Uncle Jakey's the best!" At least someone in this family appreciated me.

"He'll be a good Daddy one day." Hillary entered the room, kissed me on the cheek, and took my hand. Her fingers were warm and wrinkly from dishwater.

I cringed. I loved the fun uncle role, and it wasn't that I didn't want kids. I didn't know if I wanted kids. But the lack of subtlety, especially after her father's question, hit me like nails on a chalkboard.

"Everyone is heading out." The hair on the back of my neck rose at Hillary's breath in my ear, and I fought the urge to squirm away.

Sofie wrapped my legs in a tight hug. "Thanks for playing, Uncle Jakey!"

"Thank *you* for playing. I would have been so bored without you! I have one hundred percent never played astronaut with someone as fun as you." Sofie giggled, and we all went downstairs to say the rest of our awkward goodbyes, my hands sweating in Hillary's raisiny grasp.

"What the fuck was that?" I asked Hillary, once we were in the darkness of the car. She held a stack of leftovers in her lap.

"What was what?" I knew she felt guilty, because she didn't comment on my language.

"Your dad, like, calling me out in front of everyone."

"Oh." The top of the leftover stack began to slide, and Hillary adjusted her grip. "I said something to my mom the other day about how I was feeling ready to start our family and she probably mentioned it to him. It's nothing. You know my dad is up-front."

I hadn't known. I'd never seen anything remotely so up-front from Alan Deckland, except his distaste for me.

Why had I put up with contempt for so long? It had felt worth it at first—something uncomfortable to tolerate for the greater good, like packing lunches for work or changing the oil in the car. But what was the reward? What did I get out of dealing with the disrespect when Hillary didn't even defend me? Somewhere along the way I'd forgotten.

A ding sounded from Hillary's phone and she looked down at the screen. "Oh, I'm ovulating," she said, totally oblivious to my snowballing thoughts, the shallowness of my breath.

It had been 12 years since our high school health teacher had forced us to watch a video on the female reproductive system, but an image of a pink anthropomorphic egg came rolling back into my brain, accompanied by a turkey-flavored nausea.

"What? Why does your phone know you're ovulating?"

Hillary shrugged and looked at me coyly. "I just want to know so I'm on top of it when we do start trying. It's good to know when the best time is for sex so your chance of getting pregnant is higher."

Suddenly another factoid from sex ed returned—studies which showed mammals perceive females as more attractive when they're ovulating—one of nature's little tricks to make more babies.

My head spun. Again, I felt manipulated—by Hillary, by her family, by my own mammalian instincts, even by Sofie—what about what *I* wanted? Why did it feel like a game everyone was trying to beat me at?

"Is that why you're pretty? I thought you wanted to look nice for your family, but you're pulling some Discovery Channel egg dropping shit."

"What?" Hillary looked equally alarmed and confused.

"Hillary," I started. "I don't even know if I want kids. You know this." I put the keys in the ignition but didn't turn them. "We aren't even engaged yet and you've got your fallopians mapped out like a water park or some shit. --Ride's open today. Slippery tubes. Make sure to come back tomorrow too."

"Jake—"

"And I think it's really fuckin' weird you and your parents act like we're all on some mission to get us married."

"Jake." Hillary turned to face me and set the leftovers to the side of her in the seat. The top container slid again, landing on the floor, but Hillary didn't pick it up. "I'm sorry about my dad, but we've been together almost a decade. I'm almost thirty. You know I want kids. I don't want to pressure you, but it would be nice to at least have an idea of when…"

She trailed off, noticing my face. After years of avoiding this conversation, talking about it aloud had my fight or flight system in high gear. Hillary was more perceptive than I gave her credit for.

I was staring straight ahead, struck speechless by a realization. How had it taken me this long to understand? A life with Hillary would mean a life of these stupid parties, a life of knowing I wasn't good enough, a life of trying not to fight about how different we were. It wasn't the manipulation bothering me, although it was definitely off-putting. I didn't want to marry Hillary whether I felt coerced into it or not. For all these years, I had been using her enthusiasm for our relationship as an excuse to be less enthusiastic. I'd pushed her away with jokes and deflection and told myself it was because she tried to pull me close. When it came down to it, it didn't matter what she, or her family, did to encourage us to take the next step. I just didn't want to. Our backgrounds and personalities were just too different.

"I-" I started. Hillary looked at me, her eyes wide. "I don't want to marry you. I'm so sorry."

Hillary scanned my face, her own eyes searching for a hint of humor, or maybe uncertainty. Finding neither, she took a breath and without a word, unbuckled her seatbelt, got out of the car, and walked back into her parents' house, leaving me alone in the dark.

Shit.

I sat in the quiet, my body buzzing with what had just happened, and waited for tears, expecting them. I'd always been a crier whenever I had big emotions. And I had been with Hillary for years—I cared about her. But no tears came; the only feeling I could identify was a lightness in my chest. I looked to the Decklands' house, where warm light still filled all of the windows. Guilt struck as I pictured Hillary inside, her parents comforting her as she told them what I'd done. But there was no regret in my heart, only sympathy.

Soon though, my thoughts grew jumpy and anxious. What was I supposed to do now? Not even in the long-term sense of the question—I would have to figure that out eventually too—but what was I supposed to do *right now*? The plan had been to spend the next two nights here.

Home. I would drive home and go from there. I started the car, then paused. I would need music to keep me awake for a seven hour drive alone. Something upbeat, happy. Ska. I could listen to ska now, whenever I wanted, without disapproving looks.

Relief flooded my body as I reached for my phone to open the music app, my anxiety shifting to excitement. And it was after Thanksgiving now—I could listen to *Happy Skalidays*. Hell, I might listen to it on repeat for the next seven hours straight. It would feel good to be reminded of a time when I felt sure of who I was, who I wanted to be.

I typed "Agents of Ska" into the app's search bar and looked, but the album didn't come up. *Weird.* I selected a random ska playlist instead, then eased away from the curb, past the row of identical stucco houses toward the freeway and turned the volume up as I went, Hillary and her family fading into the distance behind me.

But even as the number of blocks between us increased, their faces stuck with me.

Sure, Alan Deckland could go fuck himself, along with all of Hillary's prissy aunts and uncles. Belinda, I mostly felt sorry for. I pictured her, meek and anxious, fussing over her only daughter, certain she'd failed at marrying her off.

The next face to appear in my mind was Sofie's. Shit. My breath caught in my throat as I realized I wouldn't get to watch her grow. What would they tell her had happened to Uncle Jakey? The thought of her defenseless at the next family outing was almost enough to make me turn around.

But I couldn't stay with Hillary to protect Sofie. I had to hope my influence was enough, at least until she grew comfortable with her own voice. She would, hopefully, get out of her sheltered bubble at some point and see how off-the-rails her family was.

And Hillary. As annoyed as I was with Hillary and her scheming, as incompatible as we both knew we were...Hillary had still been my primary companion for the last nine years.

She was the one who'd kissed my cheek after I walked across the stage at college graduation and the one who had helped me prep for my first job interviews. She was the one I'd complained to when I got rejected from one after another, and the one who'd assured me I would find the perfect employer, even if she did think it was because her Christian God was looking out for us.

Hillary and I had always been a weird match, and her faith had always made me feel icky, but there had been plenty of good parts too. Now, as I merged onto the freeway, my future felt as chaotic and unpredictable as the several lanes of post-Thanksgiving traffic.

I would focus on the songs. I wouldn't think about any of it. All I had to do was drive and listen.

The music evoked the exact same emotions they had at 17—all the adolescent angst over whether I actually should go to Berkeley, or whether I should listen to my heart and stay in SoCal with Sailor, however much it disappointed my mother, and the smarter, more responsible part of myself. Sailor. There she was, popping into my mind again. But this time, instead of pushing it down, I let the memories wash over me. I had forgotten what letting myself think about Sailor felt like in my body—the fluttering, open feeling in my throat, the tingle at my temples.

As the songs played on, I remembered her smile, the disbelief someone as cool as she was could like someone as dopey as me, that someone as pretty as Sailor could find me attractive. The desperation not to prove her ideas about me wrong. The certainty I would never love someone with as much intensity, as much excitement, as much fun and certainty as I had loved her.

Maybe I had been right. The thought made it hard to breathe. How could I have thought I could be happy with Hillary when Sailor and I had made such perfect sense? But Sailor was long gone; we had broken up for a reason. In the years since our final show, I'd pictured her outburst again and again, using the memory as evidence.

I wondered if she still went to ska shows.

Nah, Jake. Sailor was a decade ago. You have to figure out happiness on your own, but music is a good start. Turning the volume up again, I let the sound fill me, losing myself in the passing headlights and the sweet horns.

NOVEMBER 30, 2012

JakeTheB@ndG33k: Sonia's new sax line is sweet

xDrummerChickx: Not as sweet as Skankin' Kiddos finally having a new song

JakeTheB@ndG33k: not as sweet as kissing you

xDrummerChickx: that was fun too ;)

JakeTheB@ndG33k: you get me, Sailor. like all the parts… the music parts, the math nerd parts, even the silly stuff like screaming when I hear a good horn line. You get me.

xDrummerChickx: Those parts are all fun

JakeTheB@ndG33k: even my ability to sing along to Hot In Herre?

xDrummerChickx: not that lol

JakeTheB@ndG33k: You're fun too. Also! Agents of Ska has a holiday album

xDrummerChickx: Holiday like Christmas?

JakeTheB@ndG33k: yeah, but it's good even if there's nothing for us explicitly lol. But for real it is pretty cool you get the Jewish parts of me too. Most people don't

xDrummerChickx: night Jake ☒

JakeTheB@ndG33k: ☒

⋆⁎ ⋆⁎ ⋆⁎ ⋆⁎ ⋆⁎

CHAPTER 3: SAILOR

By the next morning, I'd calmed down. It was an album, not some metaphor for how perpetually abandonable I was.

Now was time to focus, recenter, move forward—all the things Rainbow would tell me her tarot cards advised. I wished they could tell me what happened to *Happy Skalidays*. I was already awake, three tabs deep in research, when Roger padded into the kitchen at his usual early hour, a sleepy Frenchie tucked under his arm. I didn't look up.

"Morning?" It was more a question than a statement as Roger set Desmond on the floor and the pup waddled over to her food bowl.

I was still hurt, but a night of sleep had given me perspective. I knew my pain was mostly rooted in fear, and I wasn't a person to give in to fear. Roger was doing what he needed to do, and so should I.

"Hey." I gave him my best amicable smile, hoping to assure him he was off the hook.

"What's this?" Roger draped his arms around my neck and peered over my shoulder to my laptop screen.

"Wanted ads. For drummers." I scrolled to the top of the page. It was LA's Craigslist, the "artists" section. In the search bar, I'd typed "drummer."

"LA?" Roger asked.

"I could commute."

"That's a lot of gas money."

"Maybe I'll get a place out there."

"Do you know how much LA rent is?"

Part of me had thought Roger would be proud at this initiative. He'd never prodded me to hustle, never been one to push, but still, I'd expected him to be encouraging. Why did I feel like he was trying to poke holes in my efforts? I could feel my anger from Thanksgiving bubbling up again, my shoulders tensing and my jaw clamping shut.

Roger leaned further over me and moved my hand from the track pad, scrolling as he read the listings aloud. "Female drummer needed for anime themed band...Stoner metal band needs drummer, bassist...Drummer wanted for True American rock album." I'd clicked on each of the listings, turning the links purple, and they were each as bad as they sounded.

I slammed my laptop shut, nearly snapping Roger's fingers off in the process, and looked at him closely for the first time that morning, his hair pressed flat on one side from sleep, his coordinating blue striped pajama set rumpled.

The coffee machine began its scheduled burbling from the counter.

"Honey." The tenderness in Roger's eyes, usually comforting, felt patronizing.

"It's not supposed to be easy," I said. "You have to work for it. I'll work for it. I've never been afraid of putting in work."

But even as I spoke, I knew how thin my voice sounded. I didn't want to be the token woman in an anime band. And even if I did, I wasn't naive enough to think the gig would lead to anything. Fame as a musician was elusive, and besides—fame was never what I'd wanted.

All I wanted—all I'd ever wanted, was to play music I loved and have enough money to get by. My best bet was to find something I was passionate about and do it on a small scale, not try to work my way up in a shitty band an hour away. I rubbed my eyes, which were dry from squinting at the screen.

"I was thinking," Roger said. Behind us, Desmond scraped her empty bowl across the floor. "You could take over my job."

I met his eyes, which were wide and imploring. My first instinct was to laugh, but there was no hint of sarcasm on Roger's face.

"I've never taught officially before. I don't have a teaching credential."

Roger put his hands on his hips. "Do you not remember me complaining about all the work I put in for my credential when I ended up at a private school and didn't need it?"

"Oh yeah." I did remember. He'd almost turned down the offer for a gig at the public Upland High, but he had student loans, and the salary couldn't compete.

"Your degree, plus your experience in marching band and teaching lessons would be enough, I think." He scratched his head. "And of course I'd be a reference."

My associate's in music had taught me enough to read music and teach others to read it.

For a minute, I let myself picture it. It was tempting...very tempting. I'd have enough money to pay rent on my own, I'd get to play music and hang out with former students. My shoulders loosened. It was comforting to realize this was what Roger had had in mind for me—taking over his job—moving forward, not backward.

I could quit my waitressing gig and probably have enough time and energy to play in a band on the side. This could be the opportunity I'd...wait.

Roger had watched me closely as I considered all of this and of course, my best friend knew me well enough to tell exactly what I was thinking. "You'd barely have to interact with Hillary at all."

But I knew Roger, too, and I knew the quirk in his eyebrow meant he was fibbing. I had somehow managed to avoid both Hillary and Jake up to this point, though I still occasionally engaged in some light social media stalking, and I wasn't about to seek either of them out.

"I don't think it's a good idea." I stood. Desmond raised her eyes toward me and I bent down to pat her head. She grunted in appreciation.

The coffee machine beeped and Roger sighed. "Think about it."

"Sure." We both knew I wouldn't.

"Want a cup?" Roger set an "I hate Mondays" mug onto the counter and lifted the carafe.

"No thanks." I was anxious enough—I didn't need to add jitters.

Roger shrugged and, caffeine in hand, shuffled back to his room to get ready for the day, leaving me alone in the kitchen with the dog.

"What do you think, Des? Am I hopeless?"

Desmond wagged her stump.

***

Though his school was closed for the holidays, Roger had been in his classroom for hours prepping things for his replacement, and the day dragged along. I wasn't scheduled at the diner, nor did I have any lessons, so I had hours to mope and scheme. Since *Happy*

Skalidays wasn't an option, I put my other favorites on shuffle and alternated between pacing and planning.

"Drum lessons. Specializing in ska and reggae," I typed in bold font, then added a graphic yoinked from the Internet—a silhouette of someone in the signature ska dance pose—a skank—one leg kicked out in front of them, the other bent behind. Below the picture, I typed my phone number.

I would go to The Barn. Maybe someone there would remember me—hopefully enough to let me hang up a flyer, but not enough to remember my freak out. Maybe I would find the man who'd organized the show—he had been a ska fan. Was it Elmer? No, that wasn't quite right. Elgin. That was it. If I remembered correctly, he'd bought copies of all of Agents of Ska's albums before the show. Did he still have them?

I shook my head to clear it. Memory was weird—how a traumatic event could lead each detail to remain in your brain, clear as day, a decade later.

On my computer, one song ended and another began—"She Won't Ever Figure It Out" by Big D and the Kids Table—and I stood, dancing over to the hook where my keys hung. I only danced like this when I was alone, lifting my shoulders and doing little hops, my head bopping as I hit "print" and the sounds of my inkjet joined the melody.

From the corner, Desmond stared at me with her dopey Frenchie face. I couldn't resist. "Come here." She trotted over and licked my ankle. I lifted her to my chest and continued dancing. I laughed as her wrinkles jiggled. As much as the music bubbled in my body, making me feel relaxed and optimistic, the more the band repeated the titular lyrics, the more they seemed to be mocking me, asking how naive I could really be.

There was no way Elgin still worked at The Barn. He'd seemed old when we were in high school, so surely he'd moved on by now. Subdued, I placed Desmond gently back on the ground. They probably wouldn't even allow someone unassociated with the college to put up a flyer.

But, as it so often did, the music gods spoke to me through shuffle as the song ended. MU330 burst into their signature "psycho ska" sound— high energy, goofy ska punk, the vocals smooth over the raucous instruments. I grabbed the flyer from the printer and clenched my keys in renewed determination as I headed to the door, letting the song play its way into chaos behind me.

★ ★ ★ ★ ★ ★ ★

CHAPTER 4: JAKE

Home didn't bring much clarity. I lowered the volume on my music as I pulled into the garage because the sound didn't fit the surroundings. Even in the Hillary-less hush, the space felt haunted by the pink cruiser bike hanging on the wall and then, inside, the decor she called "farmhouse chic"—all white and worn wood.

I was woozy—exhausted and overwhelmed at my sudden shift in circumstances. I almost felt stoned.

I stood in the kitchen, feeling the subtle shift of the space, like even the walls had turned on me. In the cabinets, I knew Hillary's ivory dishes sat in neat stacks. Her Greek yogurt and organic fruit mocked me from the refrigerator. "Jake!" I pictured them calling. "Get your fat ass out of here." I smirked, despite how lost I felt.

Too drained to deal, and still picturing asshole anthropomorphic health food, I clomped up the stairs without bothering to take off my shoes. The bedroom was no less Hillary than the rest of the house, but if I was going to think clearly, I needed sleep, so I threw myself face first onto the puffy white comforter, disturbing the stack of pillows at the head of the bed so they fell like fluffy dominoes onto my back. I barely moved. Sleep pulled at me like some tentacled sea creature.

I would take good sleep over sex, I thought, trying to ignore the little voice telling me sex might not be on the table anytime soon. Ah well. Sleep was enough.

Vaguely, I felt drool begin to pool on the blanket, but before I could make a conscious decision to shut my mouth, I was out.

When I woke, disoriented, the world came back in pieces. I was in my bed, at home, but something was wrong. My shoes were on—definitely weird, and Hillary wasn't here. I wasn't supposed to be here either. Right.

I shivered, remembering we had turned the heat off for the weekend, and peeled myself to standing. In the bathroom, I took in my reflection—my sheet-creased cheeks and wild hair, the circles under my eyes. Dammit. All my toiletries were at the Decklands'. I really wanted to brush my teeth.

Okay, I told myself. You are a grown ass man. You can go to the drugstore and buy a toothbrush. This is not an emergency.

None of this was an emergency. People broke up every day. I would handle this whole situation one step at a time. First, I'd change my clothes. The ones I had on were wrinkled and sweaty, and way more formal than I liked. It was a miracle I'd been able to sleep in them.

Without unbuttoning my shirt, I pulled it over my head and tossed it to the floor, then looked back into the mirror. I was a big guy; I always had been, and I'd learned, mostly, how to feel comfortable in my body, but now, staring at myself, I felt a flash of doubt. Maybe Hillary had been doing me a favor by dropping hints about my weight. Maybe she'd been doing me a favor by being with me at all.

No. I shook my head. I was funny and smart. I was generous and kind. I knew a person's physical appearance was the least important aspect of attraction. Besides, Hillary was objectively gorgeous, so if looks were what mattered, wouldn't I have cared more about making things work?

Returning to the bedroom and sifting through my clothes, I considered what to wear. Did I even have a style anymore? In high school, I had lived in baggy jeans and band t-shirts, but I'd given most of those up when Hillary and I got together. Except....my hand paused on a black t-shirt, tucked away on the far side of the closet, between a shirt from my office's charity baseball game and one from the beach trip Hillary and I had taken for college graduation.

The shirt felt like a living thing as I slipped it over my head, like it was fusing itself to my body like I was Jim Carrey in *The Mask*. In an Agents of Ska shirt, I could imagine I was my old self, before growing up made me boring and cynical.

Sailor had bought the shirt for me when the band was a point of connection, before everything had gone wrong.

In spite of the turn our relationship took, I hadn't been able to throw the shirt away, and had held on through multiple rounds of closet purges. Amazingly, it still smelled like trombone slide grease, and the scent transported me. Marching band. Music. Sailor.

Suddenly, my fruitless search for *Happy Skalidays* the night before came back. I must have been distracted by everything that had happened. Surely I had mistyped the album name or skipped over the result. It would be right there, like always, along with the rest of the band's discography.

But when I tried again, mind clearer from a night of deep sleep, I still came up empty. I tried another site, then another, and....nothing. Fuck brushing my teeth. I needed to find this album. I wanted to be myself again. I wanted to listen to *Happy Skalidays*.

I re-ordered my mental list. Regardless of my feelings, oral hygiene should probably come first. Not everything about adulting was overrated. So, I'd do teeth, then album, then...figure out my life.

***

The fluorescent-lit toothbrush aisle at the drug store offered a surprising number of options, and I patted myself on the back for picking one relatively quickly.

"What do you think?" I asked, holding up two toothpaste boxes to an elderly woman next to me. "Whitening? Or cavity prevention?" She looked at me warily. "You're right," I said. "Whitening is probably a scam. I'll go with cavity prevention."

I went through the motions of paying on autopilot, barely clocking the clerk's comments on the weather, still running on muscle memory as I got into my car and drove away, considering how to approach my search. The local record stores might have it. I'd check Doctor Strange first, then Rhino, and then if I had to, I'd drive to Riverside and check Rat Hole. Driving to LA sounded less than appealing, but if I had to go to Amoeba, I would.

By the time I realized I had passed the exit to my house, I was already less than a block from the first store. Oh well. I could brush in the bathroom or something. I'd been ignoring my gut instincts for too long, and my subconscious said this album was important. For once, maybe I should listen.

CHAPTER 5: SAILOR

My mind raced the whole drive to Riverside as thoughts of Roger, of Rainbow, and of next month's rent competed for dominance. Moving back in with Rainbow would make it easier to look out for her, and it would mean fewer trips across town, but I was pretty sure whatever I saved in gas I would pay for in sanity. I pushed it all down, focusing on my mission instead. Somehow, it seemed, if I could do this, prove I was capable of taking care of one small thing, then it would prove I could take care of everything. I could get my life together.

I parked in a freshly-paved lot, then hurried, practically running, past students on the sidewalk, a listlessness in their eyes I recognized from my own student days—the weirdness of the liminal weeks between Thanksgiving and winter break that directly contrasted with the urgency of final papers and exams.

They looked like babies, nothing like the cool, mature students we'd seen when we played here. The jasmine bushes lining the walk were dormant now, the sweet smell I remembered from the spring so long ago nonexistent.

Jake would have been one of those kids at Berkeley—the ones who don't go home for the shorter holidays. Had he ever missed me during those weeks?

Outside The Barn, I passed people eating thick steak fries and green salads, then stopped, paused before the door, and took a breath. This was it. The moment of truth.

Inside, it smelled exactly the same, like cheap burger patties and industrial floor wax, though the furniture looked new, and the stage curtains were dusty, like no one had held a show here in a long time. The exposed beams of the ceilings remained, but the walls had been painted, and aside from the curtains, the place felt too sterile, too clean. Taking another fortifying breath, I walked one step toward the counter, and prepared to recite the words I had practiced in the car. "Does Elgin still work here?"

Even if he didn't, I'd decided, I would use the question as a segue into my flyer-hanging request.

But the scene differed from the one I'd envisioned. The employees all appeared to be students themselves, TVs behind them displayed the menu digitally, and the mumble rap on the speakers was aggressively unintelligible. Confronted with the years elapsed since my last visit to this space, my throat tightened, and I felt unable to form the words.

"Can I help you?" asked the woman at the register as my eyes flitted from her perfectly contoured cheeks to her highlighted hair, and down to her crop top and baggy jeans. Her outfit could have been lifted from a punk kid from my own student days, but the woman at the register was clearly not an outcast. The incongruity made me a bit dizzy.

"Are you..." I wasn't sure what I was trying to ask— maybe—"Are you a student? Are you legally old enough to work? Are you interested in buying some clothes I've been stashing in the back of my closet for several years?"

"What?" The woman's expression was somewhere between annoyed and confused.

"Never mind. Sorry." Without waiting for a reply, I fled the counter.

"Sorry. Excuse me," I muttered as I squeezed between people in the line which had formed since my arrival. Their faces ranged from confused to concerned to amused. I avoided eye contact as I raced to the bathroom.

I would sit and take some breaths, drink some water, get it together and try again. The bathroom here had always been gender neutral, I remembered as I reached the door, a fact that comforted me both because the underground music scene had always been ahead of its time, and because the sign hanging at eye level had remained unchanged. I exhaled, turned the handle, and pushed open the door.

"Fuck!" A man's voice called out and the door bounced shut again.

"Oh my God! I'm so sorry. Are you—" From the other side of the door I could hear the man continue to curse. Why did that voice sound familiar?

It must have hit him at the same time it hit me, because he stopped mid-obscenity and slowly pulled the door back open.

"Oh my God," I said again. It couldn't be. My heart felt frozen in my chest. I tried to move my mouth to say more, but it felt stuck.

"Oh my God," the man in the bathroom echoed.

This was not just any man. It was Jake Rosenblatt, standing a foot away from me, his eyes the same deep brown they had always been, the sight of them squeezing my chest like someone had overtightened a drum key.

Also, he was bleeding.

"Shit." The sight of blood snapped me out of my stupor. I pushed past him to the toilet paper, unspooled a wad, and handed it to him.

"Thanks." He held it to his chin. "I think it's coming from my mouth though." Indeed, blood trickled out as he spoke.

"I didn't know you were there. I'm so sorry. But how did it..." I trailed off, trying to understand how the door had caused this kind of injury.

"I was brushing my teeth." Jake motioned toward a now-bloody toothbrush lying on the floor.

I glanced at the sink and noticed a new tube of toothpaste there, the box still beside it.

He looked sheepish. "And looking in the mirror." I turned to follow his gaze and saw the full length mirror hanging on the back of the door. "You know. Checking myself out. It's hard to resist when you look this good."

I was too stunned to laugh, though part of me registered the same goofy humor he'd always had. "Jake," I said, finally, acknowledging it was, in fact, him. "You look..." My first instinct was to say "Great," because he did, in fact, look great. He looked like the best version teenage him could have grown into, meaning he looked exactly like himself, except slightly bigger, older, something even softer and kinder about him...also bloodier. "Like a vampire." I finished instead. "Are you ok?"

"Sailor." He grinned his gap toothed grin, and if it hadn't been covered in blood, the shock of recognition might have made me faint. "Yeah, I'm fine. Thank God for the Ashkenazi genes, you know? Think the nose protected me from the brunt of it."

Now we both cracked up. I'd been avoiding Jake at Roger's concerts for years, the knowledge of him in the same space enough to put me on edge. But now, this close, I wondered what I'd been afraid of. He felt exactly like I remembered.

"Here, sit down." I reached for his arm without a thought and our eyes met for a moment before we both looked away. I closed the toilet lid and guided him down.

"I think it stopped." Jake unspooled more toilet paper and tossed the bloody bit in the metal trashcan.

"Does it hurt?"

"A little," Jake admitted, prodding his cheek with a finger. "Not bad. I'll be alright. I guess that's why you don't brush your teeth in a public restroom."

"Also why you lock doors."

Jake's smirk filled me with as much pride as it always had. God, we had loved making each other laugh.

"Let me buy you lunch," I offered, desperate to distract myself from that train of thought.

My eyes darted around the space—anywhere but Jake's face. The bathroom had once been plastered in stickers. Now there were bare tile walls and a full soap dispenser.

But if the Barn was disorienting with its weird combination of old and new, the sight of Jake—both familiar and changed—was starting to make me feel a little unhinged.

The album disappearing already felt like a joke the universe was playing on me; literally bumping into the person it reminded me of was next level. I needed to keep my head or I'd end up more off-track than I'd started.

"Really not necessary," Jake stood and rinsed his mouth in the sink, then used some paper towels to wipe the blood from his face as I tried not to think about how clearly I still remembered the press of his lips against mine. In the years since Jake, I'd kissed a few people, but none of those kisses had been so infused with emotion.

"I insist," I said, though my money situation was a big part of the reason I was here. But I owed Jake, at least for the toothbrush I'd ruined. I told myself the offer had nothing to do with the fact lunch would mean time together—the first in a decade. "Or at least let's ask an employee for some ice."

The contoured woman at the counter suppressed a smirk as we approached, apparently remembering my previous lack of composure.

"Can we get a cup of ice?" I asked, and she nodded, typing something into the register, her eyes still mocking. I turned to Jake, urging him to order.

"Ummm...I'll take a burger and...you know, fuck it." He threw his hands up in resignation. "I'd fuck with some fries, too."

"I'll have a Greek salad," I said.

"Anything else?" the woman asked. In three minutes of being around Jake, I had again almost forgotten the reason for this visit.

"Does...Elgin still work here?" I asked.

The woman cocked her head to the side, eyebrows drawn close together. "You know Elgin?" She looked like she might laugh. Details of the man returned to me—his old-timey speech patterns and looming presence. She probably thought it would explain a lot about me—of course the woman who ran away from the lunch counter and then bloodied someone's nose would be a friend of Elgin's.

"No, not really. I wanted to ask him about putting up a flyer." When she didn't respond, I added, "and ask him about a CD he used to play here a lot."

"No way," Jake said.

I snapped my head away from the woman and stared at him. "You..."

"I tried to listen to it yesterday."

"Me too. But it was just..."

"Gone," Jake finished, miming "poof" with his hands.

The woman at the counter cleared her throat.

"Sorry," we said simultaneously. Quickly, I tapped my card and waved off the receipt.

"Elgin's in the back," the cashier said, her expression friendlier as she took in my generous tip. "He loves music. Once he gets going on an album or a band, it's impossible to get him to turn it off. The last artist he got into was Olivia Rodrigo. I swear the man has the most eclectic tastes." She laughed and handed me a number for the table, then filled a paper cup with ice cubes and gave it to Jake. "I'll go get him."

DECEMBER 1, 2012

xDrummerChickx: Thanks again for the CD. It is really good!

JakeTheB@ndG33k: Right??

JakeTheB@ndG33k: I really really like you, Sailor

xDrummerChickx: I know

JakeTheB@ndG33k: that's it? Lol

xDrummerChickx: I really like you too

JakeTheB@ndG33k: that kiss after band practice was perfect. It just felt…I dunno…like one of those epic drum endings with the cymbal and everything?

xDrummerChickx: a crash out. It did feel like one.

JakeTheB@ndG33k: Like we'd been building up to it since the beginning

xDrummerChickx: I wish the album had a Hannukah song

JakeTheB@ndG33k: "All I want for Christmas….is Jews"?

xDrummerChickx: lol "I don't celebrate at Christmas. The only one without a tree."

JakeTheB@ndG33k: "I don't care about the presents. I just want Chinese to eat"

xDrummerChickx: "I just want some fried potatoes, more than you could ever know…Make my wish come true."

JakeTheB@ndG33k: "All I want for Christmas…is Jews."

xDrummerChickx: lol I'm actually here singing this

JakeTheB@ndG33k: me too!

xDrummerChickx: we should teach the band. You think Hillary would sing it?

JakeTheB@ndG33k: She's not so bad. At least not as bad as I expected

xDrummerChickx: She wears sweater vests.

JakeTheB@ndG33k: lol fair

xDrummerChickx: then again you wear those stupid sneakers even though you've never done a sport in your life and I still like you

JakeTheB@ndG33k: those were limited edition, thank you very much

xDrummerChickx: nvm, I take it all back. Even the liking

JakeTheB@ndG33k: lol

★·★·*★·*★·*★·*★·*

CHAPTER 6: JAKE

This was was some sci-fi shit. Sailor had materialized, like the image of her following me from the moment I entered campus had come to life, had defied the laws of time and space and literally pushed its way into my presence. She looked exactly the same. Or at least I'd thought so in the first moment when her face appeared in the bathroom doorway, startled and apologetic.

Now we were sitting at a table outside with the sun at my back so Sailor squinted slightly, I could see the little creases by her eyes, the slightly sharper angle of her cheekbones. She looked incredible.

I started to tell her as much. "You look..." I paused. Would a compliment be inappropriate? Considering how things had ended between us, I didn't want to risk it. "The same," I finished.

"Thanks?" Her shoulders, which I now realized had been inching toward her ears, sagged. "I guess not a lot has changed in a decade."

"Not in a bad way," I added quickly. She'd wanted things to stay the same and it had been our undoing. The last thing I wanted was for her to think I was dragging up old wounds.

Sailor's head tilted.

"I mean the same, like physically."

The corner of her mouth twitched as her eyebrows raised. I was making this worse.

I sighed. "You look fucking amazing, Sailor. You really do."

Sailor rolled her eyes, but I saw the slight blush of her cheeks as she busied herself with her salad.

"What have you been up to, dude?" I could get this back on track. I knew how to be normal. Normal people would catch up after so many years apart.

Sailor's chewing slowed. She put down her fork and swallowed.

"Honestly? Pretty much the same." She had steeled herself—her shoulders square and her eye contact direct.

"Cool. Same is cool." *Trying too hard now, Jake.*

"Yeah. Still living with Roger." Pain flashed across her face. "Teaching drum lessons."

Did she know I knew he was leaving?

"Drum lessons! That's incredible! Wow, that sounds perfect for you."

Sailor smiled, but it didn't reach her eyes. "Yeah. Living the dream." She picked up her fork and speared a cherry tomato.

"You wanna talk living the dream?" I asked, placing my elbows on the table. "I'm...wait for it...a paralegal!" I spread my fingers and shook them in jazz hands. Sailor laughed and popped the tomato into her mouth.

I tried to focus on lunch, but I couldn't stop telling myself I wasn't hallucinating—I was really sitting here with Sailor.

Over the years, I'd imagined a few scenarios. In one, Sailor still hated me, and she would storm out of whatever place we ran into each other, much like she had in high school. In the other, significantly less realistic, we ran into each other's arms like some cheesy rom-com. But the scenario I hated imagining most was the one where she ignored me, clocked my identity and turned the other way.

This was...none of those. It was just Sailor, and in some ways, it was even better than the times I'd imagined an emotional reconciliation.

It was real.

So was the pain in my face, and chewing wasn't helping.

I put down my burger and picked up the napkin I'd filled with ice cubes, then brought it to my face while I begged my mind to recall all the reasons Sailor and I hadn't worked. Sailor had a temper. She was stubborn. She could be selfish, and as much as she looked down on her mom for living in a fantasy world, she clung equally hard to her own irrational reality. And she was judgmental. She judged me. Even now, she was probably judging me, probably basking in how right she'd been about the boring-ass path I'd taken. She'd known over a decade ago I was never cut out for law. I knew all of the reasons, but why did I still feel like a god damn swarm of butterflies were having an orgy in my stomach? I lowered the napkin full of ice and wiggled my jaw. Nice and numb. I wished my emotions would follow suit.

Like she could feel my stare, Sailor looked up at me again. "You do, too…Look great."

The world seemed to slow as the words hit me. She hadn't said I looked the same, because I didn't. It had been ten years. Suddenly, all the things we'd missed, all because of a stupid fight, came rushing back. How many jokes had we missed? How much new music? How many personal milestones between adolescence and adulthood? We would never get any of it back. This casual catching up suddenly seemed stupid and shallow.

But there was something sweet about finding each other again, too. Sailor hadn't seen all the versions of me between then and now. But she saw this version, and she thought it looked great. I'd forgotten what approval from her felt like. I felt mist begin to pool in my eyes.

"I…"

"How can I be of service to you fine folk?"

I recognized the man who appeared between us immediately and snapped my attention back to our mission. He was over six feet tall, with Buddy Holly glasses and a long, gray beard.

"Hey, man," I said.

"We're looking for an album. *Happy Skalidays*." Sailor said it earnestly, like it wasn't bizarre to be asking a near-stranger for an album from ten years ago. Her serious face was adorable. I turned my gaze quickly back to Elgin, who smiled.

"Ah, Agents of Ska."

"Yes!" Sailor exclaimed.

"Released to but minor acclaim, relative to their larger discography." Elgin scratched his chin.

"Sounds right," I said.

"Lead singer Jimmy Danger, if I'm not mistaken."

"Yep," Sailor said.

"They played here at The Barn approximately ten years ago," Elgin said.

"Yeah." This was me.

Sailor's shoulders slumped slightly. It wasn't the best memory for either of us.

"'I'm Dreaming of a Rude Christmas.' I always enjoyed that one. Groundbreaking trombone work."

"Yes!" Sailor straightened and smiled as our eyes met.

"Alas," Elgin said, with a small bow. "I do not."

Sailor and I spoke at the same time. "Oh."

"But!" Elgin thrust a finger into the air. Sailor and I stared as we waited for him to continue. "Anthony Frondelli was a close friend of mine in college." Their guitar player.

"Oh!" we both said again, excited now.

"Oberlin Conservatory of Music, class of 1996." Dude was in his own world, staring off into the distance. "Always was a prodigy." Sailor and I shared another look and her smirk almost ended me. Instantly, I was seventeen again, desperate to make her laugh, to make her happy, her amusement enough to send me into my own hysterics.

I imagined the impression I'd do of this guy later. I'd straighten my posture, let my face go a bit slack. If I got my hair wet, would it be long enough to evoke his Merlin vibe? What was I doing? This was getting out of control way too quickly.

"Elgin," I said, trying to interrupt my own thoughts along with his ramblings. His eyes shot to me. "Do you know how we can get ahold of Anthony?"

"Well, I don't partake in smartphone technology," Elgin started, his gaze beginning to drift again.

"But?" I prompted.

"But he used to participate quite frequently in our class email list. I could put out some feelers."

"Yes!" Sailor said. "Do that! Put out feelers."

Elgin bowed again. "My pleasure, lass."

Somehow Sailor managed a straight face as she thanked him, wrote her number on the back of a napkin, and slid it his way.

"Of course." Elgin took the napkin. "I'll be in touch with any news."

"Thanks."

Elgin stood awkwardly for a moment, staring at us with a slight smile on his lips.

"Well, man, we'd better go." I stood and began gathering our lunch detritus, including the napkin soaked in freezing cold water and the cup with now-mostly-melted ice.

Sailor nodded and stood. "We'd better."

While Elgin remained by the table, Sailor and I backed away toward the trashcans, where we deposited our garbage.

"Thank you!" Sailor called out again before taking my arm and breaking into a sprint. Her hand grasping my elbow, we ran, bushes scratching my jeans, until we reached a sidewalk.

"That wasn't an approved exit." I rested my hands on my knees, panting. Students parted around us without acknowledgement as Sailor erupted into giggles. My cheeks twitched as I straightened, but attempting to repress my own guffaw was useless. I snorted, and a man with earbuds and a buzzcut side eyed me as he passed, which was enough to bring Sailor to a full-on cackle. It was minutes before either of us could catch our breath enough to speak.

"Oh my God," Sailor finally wheezed.

"That guy," I said.

"But maybe he'll put us in touch with Frondelli?" Sailor was still tittering.

"I wouldn't count on it." Sailor's face fell and I regretted the words immediately. "But this just means we'll have to find him ourselves," I added, embarrassed at how desperate I was to see her smile again.

She rewarded my efforts with a grin before reining her emotion in. "I guess so." Her eyes darted to the ground.

Shit. I was an idiot. I had no claim to any of the fruits of her happiness. I was lucky she was even talking to me, let alone laughing with me. Why would I push it?

Tentatively, she went on. "Will Hillary mind?"

My lips rose in a slow smile, which I quickly adjusted to an appropriately solemn expression. "We broke up." I didn't mention how recent a development this was. I also didn't let myself look into her question. There had always been tension between Sailor and Hillary, even when they put it aside for the band; of course she wouldn't want to stir anything up.

Sailor's eyebrows shot up. "Uh...oh," she stammered. "I'm...sorry?" She corrected her questioning tone. "I'm sorry. Really. That must have been rough."

"It's ok. I mean, yeah. It was a little...rough."

Was it though? Sure, it was sad...and complicated and surprising and scary. But was it rough? Any residual roughness had dissipated by the time my mouth had stopped bleeding.

Sailor watched me with concern, oblivious to her role in soothing my reeling. This was not a good train of thought.

"Where should we start?" I was fooling no one with the brightness in my voice.

I watched Sailor's apprehension shift to a smile—not the beam it had been a minute ago, but there, soft and warm.

Take it easy, Jake. I was pleading with my body to listen.

This was fine. Maybe it could be a fresh start. How dope to get a second chance to be friends. Besides, I was definitely not pursuing someone literally the day after ending a ten-year relationship. And that someone was definitely not Sailor, the person I had continuously used as the bar for the aforementioned relationship. Besides, Sailor and I had tried the dating thing and even with our chemistry, it had failed. Maybe we would have been better as friends all along. This was fine. Casual. Platonic. Fine.

★ ★ ★ ★ ★ ★

CHAPTER 7: SAILOR

My ringtone sounded before Jake could answer, and though I rushed to silence it, he knew the song instantly.

"Less than Jake." He smiled.

"Always."

"But who still has a personalized ring tone?" he teased, and for a second I was back in high school, Jake ribbing me for the time I spent applying eye liner or the $80 I blew on shoes at the mall. It was fair game, considering the shit I used to give him. That was our dynamic. He gave me a hard time and I gave him a much harder one.

"You know me—always marching to my own beat."

Jake and Hillary broke up. Jake and Hillary broke up. The words repeated in my mind like a cadence. And he'd been weird about it. He hadn't wanted to talk about it, which...sure...who wants to talk about their breakup with another ex? But still, he'd been notably weird. Right?

"I'm furious if my phone makes a sound," Jake said. "Especially if it means someone had the audacity to call me."

My laugh was feeble as thoughts of my phone call brought me back to Earth. There was only one person who called me, and talking to her was the last thing I wanted to do right now. "It's my mom. I should probably call her back."

"Rainbow!" It was the way everyone said her name—like they were recalling a joke. For other people, my mother's quirkiness was fun.

Again, I smiled half-heartedly, dreading whatever task Rainbow needed me for. "How is your mom doing?" I asked. I wanted to change the subject.

"She's..." Jake paused, his brow creasing. "She's fine, you know? She's lonely. I think she always imagined our family would be closer."

I felt a pang for Mrs. Rosenblatt, who had always been over-the-top welcoming, then another as I remembered how warm her welcome had made me feel.

"I'm sorry to hear that."

It was Jake's turn to deflect. "So I know you have to go, but how should we approach this? *Happy Skalidays.*" A curl fell over his eye, and he tossed it back with a shake of his head.

"I have no clue."

"Assuming we'll never hear from Elgin again. Can we find the band?"

"I tried," I said. "Their website is down. And there aren't exactly 'Jimmy Dangers' listed in those online directories."

"Did you try their real names?" A smile played at Jake's lips as he gave my shoulder a nudge. Again—a flash of memory.

"You know their real names?" I had only ever been aware of their alter-egos—secret agents, all with the surname "Danger." And of those, "Jimmy" was the only one whose first name I remembered.

My phone chimed again, with a text message this time. I gripped it in my purse and willed it to quiet.

"Of course I do. I spent hours reading about them. I don't remember a single thing from AP History, but Agents of Ska was Jimmy Weiner, Sammy Smith, Anthony Frondelli, Pete Honig, and sometimes Jamie West." He ticked the names off one by one on his fingers.

I stared at Jake in awe, then bemusement.

"Wait...Wasn't there a Jerome?" I was amazed the name had resided somewhere deep in my memory.

"Oh right...what was his last name? Shit."

Something else occurred to me. "And Jimmy Danger was Jewish?"

"Maybe," Jake shrugged. "Weiner. Yeah, he could have been."

"There's no way we'll find Sammy Smith—it's way too common a name, but maybe the others. You look for Anthony and try to remember Jerome's last name. I'll look for Pete and Jamie."

"What about Jimmy?" Jake asked. I thought about how starstruck I had been meeting the frontman as a seventeen-year-old, and how badly I had embarrassed myself.

"Let's try the others first," I said. An awkward silence descended and I let my eyes wander—to the trees, where birds flitted from branch to branch, and then to the parking lot, where my car waited, probably outstaying its ticket. I didn't want to leave, though. I would pay the fine, money troubles be damned.

Finally Jake spoke. "Cool. So…" He buried his hands in the pockets of his cargo shorts, his lips retaining the shape of the "o," drawing it out, as he twisted his torso from left to right.

I cut him off before he had to come up with an excuse. My cheeks flushed with the realization he was looking for an exit route. He probably pitied me. This whole "looking for the album" charade was nothing but a polite brush off, similar to the "we should catch up sometime" I gave to former students' parents when I bumped into them in the grocery store parking lot. "Yeah, you don't want to get stuck in rush hour traffic."

"No, I just meant because…Rainbow."

"Oh yeah. That too. I do need to call her back."

"But it was really great running into you even if…" He gestured toward his mouth, which had begun to swell slightly, and I winced.

"Sorry."

"I'm messing with you. I'll keep you updated on Jerome and Anthony. Your number is the same?"

"Yeah, it is. I'll look up my people too." Did he still have me in his phone? My legs felt frozen in the middle of the sidewalk, my hand still wrapped tightly around my own phone, willing whatever message awaited to be only a minor inconvenience, and recoiling at the knowledge that everything about our encounter today had confirmed the stupidity of each of my life decisions.

"Cool." Jake hesitated, like he, too, was unsure how to end this interaction. How did you part with someone you hadn't seen for ten years? What were we now? Back to friends? Acquaintances? Something else? And whatever we were, what did it mean for how we were supposed to say goodbye?

Part of me wanted to reach for Jake—to feel the solidness of him and assure myself this interaction had really happened—we'd added new notes to the song and they were better than the terrible one we had left it on.

But the last hour or so had shaken something within me, too. As calamitous as the old note had been, it had still felt final. Walking away right now felt like turning off a song during the bridge, leaving yourself aching for the release of the chorus.

My phone chimed again, filling the electric space between us and breaking the spell.

"I better go." I pulled my phone from my purse and checked the message, which was, of course, from my mother.

"Got a call from city today. Said neighbor complained about compost smell. Come help me handle?"

I sighed and resigned myself to this next task. This rendezvous had been a pleasant intermission, but who was I kidding? Even if Hillary was out of the picture, I was still stuck in a life Jake wanted no part in.

He couldn't wait to escape it when we were kids, and he certainly wouldn't want to get sucked back into it now. He'd decided an ordinary job and an ordinary life were a fine compromise as long as they got him away from me and my baggage.

He would never understand how I'd needed to reach for something—anything, however immature—to distract me from my role as mother to my own mother and the way that role tied me to one small corner of the world.

"Everything ok?" Jake asked.

"Yeah." I did my best casual shrug. "You know...the usual." *Really smooth, Sailor.*

"Sure, sure." Jake nodded and I felt the blood rise to my cheeks again. I needed to prepare myself to leave our song unfinished. There was no way he would reach out again. I should probably give up on this whole stupid search. Why would I think finding ten old songs would change anything about my life?

But wait...the album hadn't even been the main reason for my visit. I had completely forgotten to ask Elgin about my flyer. Sixty minutes with Jake and I was already forgetting my goals. I wasn't going back now, though. I'd find somewhere else to advertise.

"See ya." I had to force my legs to propel me away from the spot, toward my car, and away from Jake. Behind me, from the center of campus, the bell tower chimed, marking three o' clock. Tears pricking my eyes, I picked up my pace.

In the car, I dialed Rainbow's number and rolled the window down to let some breeze into the stuffy vehicle.

When she picked up, I didn't bother with pleasantries. "How do you want me to handle your compost smell, Rainbow?"

"I was hoping you could help me handle the neighbor."

"I do a lot for you, but I think I have to draw the line at hit man."

Rainbow chortled. "I was thinking more along the lines of finding a city ordinance about smell, or lack thereof. I've tried talking to him about the benefits of composting, but people are so stuck in their ways. I even offered to help him set up a bin, but he chose to yell obscenities. Oh well—the four agreements, right? Take nothing personally. His anger is about his own suffering, not me."

"I'm sure there's some kind of ordinance about smell. I'll look into it when I get home."

"Home? Where are you?"

I paused, not wanting to answer. "Riverside," I said finally.

"Ah, an appropriate city for my nautical navigator to explore."

"Alright, Rainbow." I was both annoyed at her weirdness and relieved she hadn't asked for more details about my whereabouts.

"There are a thousand ways to kneel and kiss the ground; there are a thousand ways to go home again," Rainbow said.

It could be difficult to tell whether my mother's quotes were from her own loopy brain or from her favorite Sufi poet, but this one I recognized as Rumi. Without acknowledging it, I hung up, closed the window, and headed home.

★ ★ ★ ★ ★ ★

CHAPTER 8: JAKE

For two weeks, I avoided search engines. I couldn't handle a rabbit hole of music and memories and shit, not right now. I'd made a mess with Hillary—all I needed was to make a mess of things with Sailor a second time.

I'd reached out to Hillary every couple days, trying to make sure she was ok, but so far, no response, and as far as I knew, she was still in Sacramento with her family.

And now it was the first night of Hanukkah. I dreaded the guilt trip I knew was coming, but it was still pretty nice to be heading to my childhood home for a holiday rather than to the Decklands'. At least at my mom's comments on my failures were subtle.

Mom was dressed up in a blue silk shirt and slacks when I arrived, her hair twisted into some kind of knot, her "face done," as she said, in full makeup.

"You look nice," I said as she leaned in to kiss me on the lips. I would have to tell her about Hillary. Hillary never came to Jewish holidays with me, so her absence was no surprise, but I knew if my mom found out about my breakup from someone else, she wouldn't let me live down keeping her in the dark.

"This? It's nothing. What are you wearing, Jakey? Why are you dressed like a schmuck? I hope you at least put some deodorant on."

"Gee, thanks, Ma." I looked down at my green striped polo. I wasn't dressed *that* badly. "And yes, I'm wearing deodorant." When she turned to lead me into the dining room, I took a quick sniff of my armpits to confirm. Yep. Good ol' antiperspirant.

"You're so handsome. I wish you would take some pride in your appearance," my mom called back over her shoulder.

Around the table, she had laid out enough food for five people. "I know I'm husky, but how much do you think I can eat?"

She ignored me.

"So I called the phone company yesterday afternoon because my bill went up four dollars last month. I didn't notice until yesterday when I saw my credit card statement—you know I get the paper ones because I don't trust those digital copies. I love the environment, of course, but they could change them at any time if you don't have the hard copy to file, so I have them sent the old fashioned way so I can keep my files. Anyway, I didn't see the statement until yesterday and I called, because you know me—how much do I use my phone? Sixty dollars is already ridiculous—they're going to add some fee for an old lady?"

It had begun.

"So they had me on hold for thirty minutes. And you know I worry about holding the cell phone to my ear so long because of the segment I told you about. On Dr. Oz? So I put it on speakerphone and when the representative finally picked up, the lady said she couldn't hear me. So I said, 'one second,' and the lady said 'I can't hear you ma'am.' So I shouted at her to wait a moment while I tried to figure out how to get the phone off of speakerphone, but of course by that time, she was already annoyed at me. Representatives these days have no sense of customer service. No patience. They're all young kids who have had cell phones their whole lives so they've never had to wait for anything and—"

It was no use trying to follow the rant. My mind wandered as I shook my head and furrowed my brow at occasional intervals. In some ways, Hillary and my mom were not so different. As the smell of food reached my nostrils, my stomach let out a loud grumble. *Wrap it up*, I willed my mother, but the story and its several tangents went on and on. I understood being lonely, but sometimes it felt like my mom used me as a receptacle for her complaints—a way to get every garbage thought out of her head. Finally, she took a breath, wiping her forehead like the complaining had worn her out, too.

I took the opportunity to move the night along. "Should we light the menorah?" I asked.

"You do it, honey. Say the prayer. You know I love Hebrew in your voice. If you remember the Hebrew."

"I dunno, Ma. I've only said it every year for...let's see...almost thirty years."

I went through the motions of the ritual and tried to ignore the ache in my throat as my mother's face changed, her aggravation fading to pride. So much of her identity was wrapped up in me as a good person, a good son. If she knew how mediocre I really was, she would feel like a failure.

Maybe she did know.

As I finished lighting the final candle, mom began to pile greasy latkes on my plate. Deep down, maybe she knew I was a disappointment, and maybe it was the root of her passive aggression. Maybe she cherished moments like this because she could pretend I was who she wanted me to be—a son who had made something of himself, who had married a nice Jewish girl and given her grandbabies, a son she could brag about at Temple. Better get it out of the way.

"I broke up with Hillary."

I was fully expecting a record scratch reaction. Even Christian grandbabies were better than no grandbabies.

But my mother shrugged. "Oh, well. You still have plenty of time to find someone. Here. Have some beets. You know I can't do all the sugar, even in vegetables. Beets do have a lot of sugar, you know. I told Betty the other day, 'Beets have sugar,' and she told me, 'But they'a vegetable.' As if I didn't know beets were a vegetable. They're a root vegetable. As if my grandmother hadn't brought a trunk of beets when she came from Poland. As if I didn't grow up eating beets with every meal. No wonder I'm pre-diabetic."

Huh. That had gone...better than I'd expected.

"You were half beet as a child!" I said, imitating the exact way she always ended this story.

"Exactly. Although I wish I had thought more about your diabetes risk. Ah well. A serving won't hurt you. Eat."

Later, dishes done, sprawled on the living room couch, full of latkes and beets, my mom sat in the recliner, remote in hand. She flipped channels for several minutes, then finally, turned off the TV. "There's nothing on anymore. Five hundred channels and it's all garbage."

Five hundred channels. A memory lit in my brain like a lightbulb. "Five Hundred Channels" was a Choking Victim song. When was the last time I had listened to Choking Victim? Without Hillary policing me, there were so many bands to rediscover.

I crossed the room to my mom's computer—the same one she'd had for years—in three steps. Now, it booted at a snail's pace. I tapped my fingers on the desk while I waited, remembering all the times I'd done exactly the same thing while listening to music and waiting for Sailor to message me back. I was relieved when the browser finally loaded, to find Choking Victim's discography was still intact online. I clicked on "Five Hundred Channels," the old song scratching an itch I didn't know I had.

Oof. I'd missed this song.

But a deeper itch reared its head. God, I really wanted to hear *Happy Skalidays*. It didn't have to be a big deal. It was just music. Of course, I'd send it to Sailor if I found it, but it didn't have to be a big thing. I was a grown man. I could search for whatever holiday music I wanted.

I typed "Anthony Frondelli" into the search bar. The first result was him, there was no question—a LinkedIn page listed him as a grocery store manager in Bayonne, New Jersey. I recognized the picture immediately, even without the bright blue spiked hair. Frondelli still wore thick black-rimmed glasses, and his profile picture featured the same thick-lipped smirk. I clicked on the link and only hesitated a second before clicking "message," hoping my "paralegal" title on the site would make me seem legit and not spammy.

"Hi Anthony," I typed, before deleting it and writing, "Hi Mr. Frondelli." I went on: "I'm sure you don't remember me, but I was in a ska band in Southern California a long time ago. We played with you at The Barn in Riverside. We're looking for an old album of yours."

I hit send.

A response appeared almost immediately, and I jumped like a dog at a bell. I was used to associating the site's notification sound with dreams of recruiters for one of those offices with ping pong tables and free lunches.

But this was even better—a message from Frondelli held real possibilities for a new life.

"I don't play music anymore."

Oh. The tight hope gripping my chest a moment earlier dropped into my stomach.

"I'm hoping you could help me find a copy of *Happy Skalidays*. It seems like it's disappeared from all the regular sites," I responded.

"I'm not involved in any of that. Who told you to talk to me?"

Why was this dude so defensive? I was ready to give up when I had another idea. My heart picked up speed.

"Elgin. I spoke to him recently and he said you might know where to look."

There was a pause, and I imagined Anthony thinking on the other side of the screen. Then finally, his message appeared.

"Elgin is a good man. He's one of the only ones I talk to from those days. Him and Jerome."

Oh shit! This was my in. "Could you remind me of Jerome's last name?"

There was another hesitation, then eventually, "Higgins." Then in another message, "Jerome Higgins."

"Thank you!" I typed. "Thank you so much."

"Don't contact me again," Frondelli said. "I try not to think about those days."

Super weird. I hadn't planned to contact him again, but still...weird.

"Ok."

I resisted sending a "Chill" meme and closed the tab. The conversation had left me with a strange feeling. I wiped my sweaty palms on my pants and cleared my throat before getting back to work.

"Jerome Higgins" yielded several pages of results—most from websites with names like "I-P-Q" and "Find Them." I clicked a few of these—the ones claiming to have emails and phone numbers—but they all wanted money, and they all seemed super scammy.

I wasn't opposed to spending the $29.95 to uncover the information, but who knew if any of these were the right Jerome Higgins, and besides, as much as I wanted to find the album, I didn't really want to give money to a website built for stalkers. If someone wanted to be findable, they would be findable.

Finally, I came to another LinkedIn profile—this one for a Jerome Higgins in Trenton, in human resources. I clicked the profile and scrutinized the picture. This Jerome Higgins was white. Jerry Danger was Black. I exed out of the tab.

Further down in the search results, a link from a news site seemed promising. A Jerome Higgins in Brooklyn had started a camp that helped foster kids form bands and perform. I squinted at the picture. This one was him. Yup. This was a 50-year-old Jerry Danger. There was no contact information on the article, but when I searched the name of the camp, the website popped up immediately. Across the top of the screen scrolled a blue banner with the words, "We're hiring" in white font. For a second I forgot what I'd come to the site for.

When I clicked, the loaded page read, "We're looking for a legal researcher."

Whoa. The possibility was almost too good to be true. Every day at Sparker and Sons Law Firm was pretty much the same. I squeezed into a polo and unflattering khakis so I could sit at my desk pretending to care about 500-page law books, while I watched old standup bits on my phone.

But working for a cool company, and in New York—it was the kind of life I had thought going away to school might lead to—the kind of life I had convinced myself since graduation was unrealistic. I filed the information away. I would come back to this.

The contact page listed Jerome Higgins, Executive Director, with an email address and phone number under his name. I picked up the phone to call, but stopped myself before pressing send. The sight of Jerome and Anthony, their greying hair and lined faces, had hit a weird chord. Until a couple weeks ago, Sailor and I hadn't seen each other in almost a decade.

All our bandmates—Go, Roger, Sonia, Romero—were people I used to know well, and now we kept up with each other online, like there was more to my story with them. In most cases, though, we'd probably keep vaguely following along with each other's lives, seeing one another a small, countable number of times, until we were all old.

Social media made life so weird.

I didn't want that with Sailor. I wanted a real story with her—more real story, even if it was just as friends. She was worth it. If I found the album on my own, we might not see each other for another ten. We'd be close to forty. Jesus.

No, I would stop searching for the album for now, and then maybe when we got together next time, we could try calling Jerome together. My heartbeat picked up speed as I thought about seeing Sailor again, imagining us sitting side by side to make the phone call, hugging when we found what we were looking for.

Something else stirred when I imagined the feeling of her body pressed against mine—her breasts, which had grown even fuller since high school, the warmth of her against me. It would be even better now that we were older—now we knew what we were doing—now we could appreciate what we didn't before. I would make her feel safe this time—tell her I wasn't going anywhere. I would listen to her when she didn't think something was right for me.

Ugh, the thought was almost too much—the physical and the emotional all wrapped up together. Shit. I adjusted my erection and glanced nervously over my shoulder at my mom, who was dozing behind me, her mouth hanging open, her eye makeup smudged in the corners.

Clearly, my subconscious wanted things my practical side wouldn't let myself consider. But the more I thought about it, the thinner the excuses I'd listed over and over since our run-in seemed. People got back together all the time. We'd both grown over the past ten years. I was single.

Nope. I was being a creep. That was creepy. *Stop being a creepy dude, Jake.*

Maybe I could be open to possibilities, but I needed to feel Sailor out. I was in a weird headspace, with Hillary and now this. It wasn't the best time to throw caution to the wind and move on impulse. Even if the chemistry had been mutual, it could be residual from the old days, just something my body remembered.

I would wait for Sailor to get in touch with me.

I stared at my phone on the desk, begging it to light up. Behind me, my mom let out a snore.

CHAPTER 9: SAILOR

"Who is Pete Honig?" Roger asked, startling me.

I snapped my laptop shut and looked up at him. He was less than a foot from the kitchen chair where I sat, his hands on his hips like the teacher he was. "How long have you been standing there?"

"Don't worry. If he's a porn star, I saw nothing." Roger mimed zipping his lips, then walked over to the blinds and opened them to allow the last orange bits of day to shine through. Desmond followed, flopping down into the sun spot, then rolling onto her back to soak it in. "Or should I go look him up myself?"

"He's not a porn star." I laughed. "He was in Agents of Ska."

"I knew it sounded familiar! He sounds like a porn star, though, doesn't he? Like he's got a big honig d—"

"Ok!" I cut him off. "I guess he sounds like a porn star."

"Why are you looking him up?"

Roger's conspiratorial smile shifted to a concerned half frown as I filled him in on the missing album, the run-in with Jake, and our decision to find *Happy Skalidays* together.

"Is this a good idea?" His eyebrows drew closer together.

"Oh, he and Hillary broke up. I forgot that part. Has she been weird at work or any—"

Roger took a step closer. "That's not my only concern. If they broke up, it was recent, and I don't know if being a rebound is such a great..." Roger took a deep breath and sat beside me, placing his hand over mine where it lay on the closed laptop. "Honey, Jake broke you."

The words hit like glass, their truth slicing into me. I couldn't hide my reaction.

Jake *had* broken me. But still—what right did Roger have to point it out? He was leaving me ,too. I knew he was trying to protect me, but he had lost his claim to concern. I wouldn't have even run into Jake if I hadn't gone to The Barn, and I wouldn't have gone to The Barn if Roger wasn't leaving.

"And you're doing a great job helping me stay together," I mumbled, pulling my hand out from under his.

He didn't take the bait. Roger was always the calm one, the responsible one, the reasonable one. With a sigh, he stood and kissed the top of my head.

"I'm going to go say bye to the people at Temple while they're setting up for the Hanukkah dinner. I figure I'll be too busy later. Do you want to come with me?"

I looked up at my friend—the one who knew my every quirk and whose quirks I knew, who knew my bad habits and loved me anyway. He had subsidized my living arrangements, brought me soup when I was sick, and never once failed to include me. But he was leaving. He was moving on and growing up. When it came down to the most important thing of all, he had left me out. And now he had the gall to question the way I was dealing with it?

My voice shook when I spoke. "You're not Jewish, Roger. Why are you going to the Temple? You are a gay Black man. What is with your weird obsession with Judaism? It's fucking bizarre."

A hurt I had never seen before sprung to Roger's face, twisting at my break of an unspoken agreement. Roger and I were supposed to be on the same team—us versus the world, and this was more than a petty argument.

But the words kept coming, spilling from my mouth like marbles. "In spite of what everyone seems to think, I'm not an idiot. I actually did learn some things at community college. I read about something called Philosemitism in World Religions—heard of it? You never cared about me. You probably only kept me around this long because I'm Jewish."

From the floor, Desmond let out a low rumble—not a growl, but a warning.

Roger's nostrils flared. He pursed his lips and shook his head from side to side, his gaze toward the ceiling. He was trying not to cry. "Because your preoccupation with ska isn't weird. Not appropriative at all, Sailor. The genre was totally made for suburban white girls."

The accusation hit as intended—like a punch to the gut. My best friend was standing before me, pointing out how my entire identity, the obsession I had built my life around, thrown away relationships for, didn't belong to me—could never really belong to me.

Like everything else. Everything was for other people, and the world would not let me forget it. I gaped at Roger, unable to form words amidst the shame, hurt, and anger bellowing within. My throat felt thick, and I swallowed hard. Heat flushed my whole body.

"You could have just said no," he said, finally, his voice carefully controlled. He turned around and left.

Desmond followed him to the door, whining softly, but Roger slammed it in her face.

"Come here, Des." I patted my leg as the door's reverberations quieted. But the dog walked past me, out of the kitchen. Alone, the hum of the refrigerator and the whir of the laptop's fan roared in my ears alongside my pulse.

Propping my elbows on the table, I dropped my head to my hands, palms pressing into my eyes until stars swam. So what if Roger was right? Ska was outsider music, and I had always been an outsider. I ignored the voice in my head screaming Roger probably felt the same way about Judaism.

His imminent abandonment meant he had no right to tell me what to do or not do going forward. Who the hell was he to worry someone might hurt me? He had made it clear my feelings were close to inconsequential to him. I sat up and threw my laptop back open so hard, the hinge squeaked in protest.

Leaning toward the screen until my vision blurred, I resumed my search as the kitchen grew dark. Though my chest fluttered with every potential lead, after half an hour of sifting through biographical information about numerous Pete Honigs and Jamie Wests, I resigned myself to the futility of finding the former band members. The names were too common. I bit my bottom lip, picked up my phone, and texted Jake.

"Any luck?"

JANUARY 4, 2013

JakeTheB@ndG33k: Shabbat Shalom

xDrummerChickx: Aren't you not supposed to be online on Shabbat?

JakeTheB@ndG33k: Shhh

xDrummerChickx: I'm telling the Rabbi

JakeTheB@ndG33k: lol when's the last time you went to temple?

xDrummerChickx: It's been awhile. Rainbow asked the Rabbi whether God was meant to be a literal being or if she was free to interpret it more as "the Universe"

JakeTheB@ndG33k: and she didn't like her answer?

xDrummerChickx: I think she just got bored. We went to a Quaker meeting in Claremont after, and a Unitarian place in Montclair. She even dragged me up to a zen center in Mount Baldy once for a silent meditation.

JakeTheB@ndG33k: Wow. Can't say I'm not jealous

xDrummerChickx: don't be

JakeTheB@ndG33k: but for real I logged on because Shabbat was weird tonight

xDrummerChickx: weird how?

JakeTheB@ndG33k: Roger came

xDrummerChickx: …

JakeTheB@ndG33k: his parents told him not to come back for summer break

xDrummerChickx: omg because…

JakeTheB@ndG33k: yep

xDrummerChickx: omg

JakeTheB@ndG33k: my mom brought him in and threw a kippah on his head and had him light the candles. He's sleeping on the couch.

xDrummerChickx: your mom's an angel

JakeTheB@ndG33k: I wouldn't go that far

★ ★ ★ ★ ★ ★

CHAPTER 10: JAKE

Holy shit, had I actually invited Sailor over? When was the last time she'd been here to my mom's house? It had been a decade. There was no way I could have resisted though. Her text had me drooling like a puppy, eager for more of her.

And now she was here, and also, *shit*, here was mom, insisting on greeting her at the door like we were in high school, hugging her so tight there was no way Sailor could breathe.

"Oh my *God*, Sailor!" Mom squealed before letting her go. "Oh my God, look at you. Adorable as ever."

Sailor blushed as we all looked at her dark jeans and tight black hoodie, and my own cheeks colored as I tried not to think about what was underneath. "Sorry, I didn't get to change before I—"

Mom cut her off. I was the only schmuck in her eyes. "You're perfect. Adorable. Come in."

Sailor looked back at me and smiled as I shrugged apologetically and followed them.

Mom had kept it simple when it was me and her—the clay menorah I'd made in fifth grade the only difference from her standard well-kept table. But apparently when she'd found out Sailor would be joining us tonight, she'd gone for the works.

Under Bubbie Zadie's good dishes there was an ivory tablecloth, the silverware was wrapped in navy blue napkins, and she'd traded the clay menorah for a shiny silver one I hadn't seen since...since the last time Sailor had celebrated here.

"Mom, I didn't know you were doing a whole thing. I would have helped." I felt guilty for showing up right before the time I'd told Sailor.

"Hush, Jakey. You have your own life. I didn't want to bother you. And besides, I wanted to do something nice. How often do I get to see this young lady?"

"Thanks." Sailor smiled. "It's beautiful."

Mom beamed. "Sit, sit, you two." Our chairs squeaked as we settled into them and again, I doubted my critical thinking skills. My matchmaker mother would make this super weird, and if Sailor was even slightly ambivalent about what our reunion meant, an intimate evening in the Rosenblatt house would have her running the other way.

"Jakey?" Mom handed me the menorah.

Starting on the right side, I put two blue candles into their cups, then added the shamash in the middle. Lighting the center candle first and using it to ignite the others, I began reciting the blessing, and the women joined in.

Baruch atah Adonai.

Sailor's alto voice was sweet, with the slightest hint of an edge. Watching the candles come to life, I began to relax, the tension I'd been holding in my shoulders chilling the slightest bit.

Eloheinu Melech ha'olam.

My mom's voice was practically bubbling with glee as the final words poured out like water.

Asher kid'shanu b'mitzvotav v'tsivanu l'hadlik ner shel Hanukkah.

Immediately, the space felt like a holiday, like the ritual had made the room cozy and sacred. It was so simple, lighting candles, but it really could change the vibe.

In that moment, it was like I could see into the future, the glimmering lights a crystal ball. I could see Sailor and I lighting candles next year, and the next, and all the years after. I could see our children lighting candles, smiling gap-toothed smiles, their curls lit up by the dancing flames. Suddenly, there were tears in my eyes, and I had to fight the overwhelming urge to reach for Sailor's hand.

"Now, who's hungry?" My mom's voice broke through my thoughts. I looked at Sailor before answering, and though I knew she couldn't read my mind, her gentle smile made it seem like she approved. Hope beat against my rib cage as I warned myself not to look too deeply into it.

Dinner went as expected—my mom probing Sailor for every detail of the last ten years of her life. As Sailor responded, I realized she'd really done it—avoided selling out, just like she'd planned. After getting her associate's, she began teaching drum lessons for a living.

She didn't mention any new bands, and I didn't want to know. She didn't mention any boyfriends or girlfriends either.

"You probably know Jakey and Hillary broke up." My mother had absolutely zero tact.

"Mom," I snapped.

"What? We're all getting caught up." She smiled coyly into her salad. When I chanced a glance at Sailor, she was smirking, too.

My mom spent the rest of the meal talking me up—a deranged wingwoman with too much perfume. Sailor feigned fascination as I blushed. By the time we were all done eating, I was ready to shepherd Sailor straight out the door to prevent any further damage.

"Don't you dare." Mom smacked Sailor's hand away as she tried to stack our empty dishes. "You and Jakey have fun. Let me handle this."

"Oh, Mrs. Rosenblatt—" Sailor started, but Mom cut her off.

"I won't allow it. Out." And with that, she swept the plates from the table and herded us out of the dining room.

Sailor headed toward the living room, our old hangout spot, but I knew my mom would be there and in our business as soon as she finished cleaning.

"We can go up here," I said, tipping my head toward the stairs.

"So anyway," Sailor said, once we'd arrived in my old room, where the twin bed was still covered in the same bright blue comforter I'd had since I was thirteen. Mom had decorated as my big Bar Mitzvah present, and enormous soccer ball and football decals still covered the walls, remnants from the time before I realized I was much more of a band kid than a sports kid. Even here, the candles' spell lingered, and the dark room, lit only by a desk lamp, was calm.

"The names you gave me were impossible," Sailor said. "What did you find?"

"Oh, nothing. Just a number and email address for Jerome Higgins."

Sailor swatted me on the shoulder. "You're just now telling me this?" I grinned. "Let's call him!"

"What do we say?" I had meant it when I'd said I hated phone calls.

"We want to know how to find his old holiday album."

"That's not weird?"

"Why would it be weird?"

"I don't know. I hate talking on the phone," I said.

"You've mentioned." Sailor paused. "But we used to talk on the phone all the time."

"We did." It was true. I'd spent hours with my phone between my ear and shoulder. Sailor and I would stay on the line and listen to each other breathe when we didn't have anything to say, and not once did it feel awkward. "But that was different."

"You're a baby. Give me the number."

I laughed, sitting on the bed, taking out my phone, and navigating to the nonprofit's site while Sailor sat beside me and looked over my shoulder. Her breath on my neck gave me goosebumps, making me thankful for my long pants.

"Wow! This is cool. Good for him."

I searched her face for sarcasm but found none.

"Should I do it?" I asked.

"Do it!"

I highlighted the number and my phone asked if I wanted to call. But before I could click on the green icon, a notification flashed across my screen—a message from Hillary.

I went cold as the blood drained from my face. "Shit."

"No worries." Sailor smiled unconvincingly and adjusted her gaze from the phone to her hands, leaning slightly away from me.

"Sorry." I swiped to view the text.

"My parents know a guy from church," it said. "If you and I are really over, I'm going to move up North. I'll live with my parents and meet this guy. But you have to tell me now. I love you, Jake."

This was Hillary's Hail Mary. I'd been waiting for it, and of course this was the moment she'd chosen. She was trying to give me one last chance, hoping I would say I'd made a mistake. But I couldn't lie anymore, especially not with Sailor sitting beside me like a sexy personification of my conscience.

"I understand," I typed back while Sailor drummed her fingers on her legs beside me, her gaze shifting around the room as she tried to give me privacy. "You need to do what you need to do. Go meet him."

In the message window, bubbles bounced to indicate Hillary was typing, then disappeared. I stared at it for several more seconds, then put it face down on the bed, and looked back at Sailor, who didn't ask anything. She was still glancing around, breathing slowly.

"It was Hillary," I said, and she turned to face me, doing her best to keep the emotion from her face. "She's moving up North."

"It's really over?" Our gaze held and I felt my own breathing slow.

I nodded once. "It should have been a long time ago."

"Are you...are you ok?" Sailor reached a hand toward me, then pulled it back.

"Yes," I said definitively. "Very." Now I reached out, taking her hand in mine, rubbing small circles with my thumb as we continued staring into each other's eyes. Slowly, Sailor nodded too, and before I could stop myself, our mouths were pressed together, exploring and hungry, our hands roaming up and down each other's torsos as if we could reclaim all the years we'd missed. Downstairs, dishes clinked.

"We'll have to be quiet," Sailor breathed as she wound her fingers through my hair. I nodded. Slowly, we eased back until we were lying sideways on my boyhood bed, face to face, our arms tangled and our legs hanging over the side.

"So quiet," I whispered, shoving my phone off the bed. It landed face up on the floor with a thud. As I adjusted my body to position myself over Sailor, I looked down at the screen. There was no response from Hillary.

JANUARY 14, 2013

JakeTheB@ndG33k: Today was fucking amazing

xDrummerChickx: it was awesome ⊠

JakeTheB@ndG33k: Are you doing ok? You don't regret it do you? Or like hurt or anything?

xDrummerChickx: my vag is fine but maybe doing it for the first time on top of a gas station was not the best choice. there's roof gravel like permanently embedded in my knees lol

JakeTheB@ndG33k: haha mine too. Sorry

xDrummerChickx: but it was fun

JakeTheB@ndG33k: Do you feel different? I feel different

xDrummerChickx: yeah, kind of. It's weird.

JakeTheB@ndG33k: I love you Sailor

xDrummerChickx: I love you too

CHAPTER 11: SAILOR

y eyes welled with tears as Jake leaned in to kiss me, and I kissed him back, desperately, grabbing his head with my hands, his curls between my fingers, as if I could stop myself from crying if I could get him close enough.

His hand on my arm was larger than it had been when we were teenagers. Now, it felt strong and confident and safe, but it was still Jake's hand. I turned to lie on my back, and his strokes drifted to my stomach, the weight grounding me to his bed.

Jake was the one who seemed desperate now, his kisses moving from my ears to my neck to my collarbone as I gently kicked off my Converse and shimmied out of my high-waisted jeans, letting them fall to the floor.

"I love this underwear," Jake said.

"These?" I laughed, looking down at my grey cotton bikini cut panties.

"Yes. They're simple and sexy." He slipped a finger under the top a fraction of an inch and my breath caught. For several seconds, we both watched my belly move up and down with my inhalations and exhalations, his finger remaining barely under the elastic, until I could no longer take it. There was an ache between my thighs, begging for his hands, and I wanted to touch him everywhere too—to explore all the ways he'd changed and all the ways he'd stayed the same.

I scrambled to lift his shirt, and as he sat up to help, I instantly missed the feel of his fingers, how close they had been to where I needed them. But I couldn't resist his now-exposed torso—instantly my fingers were on his chest, the hair there wound between my fingers. The roundness and broadness of him, the solidness...he was a man.

Jake resumed kissing me, his mouth everywhere—my mouth, my cheeks, my neck, my hair, and I let my fingers trail downward toward his jeans.

When I reached his button, Jake's breath hitched. "Sailor." His voice was deep and longing. He sounded like he might cry too. "Sailor, I've missed you so much."

"I know." I unzipped him and he moaned again, though I hadn't yet touched him. Moving to the floor and kneeling before him, I pulled his jeans and boxers down to the floor. He was rock hard as I took him into my mouth—the hair from his stomach continuing down around his erection, but trimmed more neatly there. I wanted to bury my face in it, breathe him in. Before I could, though, Jake was tugging at my shoulders, gently guiding me up from the floor and onto his lap, my knees straddling him, his erection throbbing against the fabric of my underwear. We kissed again, hard.

If he wouldn't let me go down on him, I wanted him inside of me. "Does your door lock?" I whispered.

"Yes, but Sailor." His brown eyes were huge and glistening, his voice gentle.

My throat tightened. Had he changed his mind? Maybe it was too soon. I had been presumptuous, assuming—

"We should put on some music. It's hard to be quiet." I exhaled as my tears broke free along with my breath.

"Aw." The tenderness of Jake's voice made me cry harder. I hated crying, especially in front of people. I lifted my eyes to the ceiling and rubbed at my cheeks with the backs of my hands. Jake cupped my face between his large hands and used his thumbs to wipe my tears until I met his gaze again.

"The Specials," I said, and watched as Jake flushed with emotion at the words. We both knew it would be perfect.

With my legs still on either side of his lap, Jake wrapped his arm around my shoulders and dipped me backward toward the floor to grab his phone. My stomach fluttered with the vestibular shift—reminiscent of playground swings and Lemon Festival carnival rides, and as he whooshed us upright my vision went briefly black.

It returned to see The Specials albums all available to play.

"Thank God," I said, and though Jake laughed, I saw his own eyes fill with tears as the familiar upbeat and trombone kicked in.

Not everyone understood the intensity of emotions music could make you feel, but we did. I knew Jake, hearing the same songs we'd listened to so many times together, felt it too— the ache of missing each other, and the sweeter ache of being here together now.

I leaned in and kissed him again as his hands explored my back, my shoulders, my waist. We kissed and kissed, like we had in high school, when making out was an activity in itself. Like then, it felt infinitely interesting, his soft lips on mine, the music taking on new dimensions as if absorbing every moment it was attached to, like it grew richer with each new listen.

I could be happy, I told myself, even if it went no further. Here, on Jake's lap, The Specials on his phone, I could be happy forever.

But Jake stopped, pulling away from me abruptly. Again, I missed the closeness immediately. Again, dread filled me. Had I done something wrong?

Wiping his own tears, Jake smiled his beautiful gap-toothed smile. "Let's lock the door."

"Fiiiiine," My tone was playful, but really, I hated the thought of pulling even further apart.

But when Jake returned to the bed, the lock securely turned, he guided me onto my back, straddling me now, his forearms flat on either side of my head, our noses almost touching, and my ache for him was replaced by gratitude for his presence.

"I don't want to hurt you," he said.

"What do you mean?" The feelings pulsing through me right now were the opposite of pain.

"On top. I'm bigger..." he paused. "I'm bigger than I was."

My head could not shake vigorously enough. I had never wanted something more in my life than I wanted the weight of Jake—all of him, on top of me—feeling me, knowing me.

"Please," was all I could manage to say, and he conceded, letting his body rest on mine, holding me firmly to the bed, to the astonishing magic of what was happening.

As we resumed kissing, Jake's hands inching up the sides of my ribs, I grew suddenly impatient. I wanted more of him, closer, faster. I had waited for this for so long and my patience was up. Greedily, I wrapped my fingers around his head and urged him downward.

Jake moved achingly slowly, first lifting my shirt over my belly button, planting kisses there, then pushing it higher and higher until it rested above my bra.

"Is this sexy too?" I smirked, nodding down toward the laundry-worn underwire covering my breasts.

"Extremely." Jake's voice was almost a purr. "But we should still take it off."

He pushed my bra up over my breasts and a small groan emerged from his throat as they appeared, his patience gone now too. In an instant, Jake's hands were on my shirt, pulling the garment over my head, which bounced back onto the bed.

I laughed, half-startled at the swiftness with which he had removed it. Tongue between my teeth, I slid my bra straps down my shoulders.

Again, Jake was quick, his hands behind me unhooking my bra and throwing it to the ground before I knew what was happening.

In another instant, Jake's mouth was on my breast, his tongue flicking until my nipple was hard and tight, and I gasped as a shiver ran from the spot where his teeth and tongue teased, right down to my groin, leaving me desperate for more touch. My muscles tensed at my body's first hint of involuntary movement.

I had never been shy about asking for what I wanted during a hookup, but now I hesitated—scared of what I might say or how I might act if I let myself really let go. I didn't have to play it cool with Jake, I reminded myself, and took his hand, placing it between my legs over my now- soaked underwear.

Jake rolled onto his side next to me, his erection pressing into my hip as he continued to explore the outside of my cotton briefs. When his fingers grazed the dip of the fabric at my entrance, Jake moaned again and moved his head to rest on my chest.

"Dayenu," he breathed, the air of it making my other nipple rock hard.

"What?" I laughed, rubbing my panties wantingly against his hand. I didn't want to talk. I wanted him to reach into my underwear.

"Dayenu," Jake said again, lifting his head to look up at me. "It would have been enough. Just seeing you again. Just kissing you. Just touching you. It would have been enough, but now this."

But I was past the point of mushy talk, my body moving steadily toward a conclusion it didn't want to delay. "It wouldn't have been enough," I responded breathily as urgency continued to grow. I arched my back and rocked my hips against him, the heel of his palm hitting a spot that seemed to eclipse all rational thought. "It's not enough." Taking his hand again, I slipped it into my panties, watching his face as he felt my wetness.

His eyes practically rolled back in his head with pleasure.

Seeing his unbridled desire unleashed my own. We would be unrestrained together. Somehow, with Jake, I could compartmentalize—fully embody the feral parts of myself, without worrying the image would overtake my carefully crafted coolness.

"Oh my God," he said, and as he slipped a finger inside of me, the sound of agreement I made was animal—somewhere between a mew and a growl.

"Shh," Jake whispered, reminding me his mom was right downstairs.

The injunction didn't quell my uninhibited enthusiasm—only lowered the volume, and the hint of command in his voice made me wetter. Pressing my lips together to quiet my moans, I let my eyes close as I felt myself contract around his finger as my body tried to hold him, claim him.

"Oh my God," I repeated, thrusting my hips and trying to feel his finger deeper, faster, his palm cupping me, bumping against me with each of my thrusts. I was an instrument Jake was playing—lying on the bed, my body spasming at each pulsing contact, while he watched in satisfaction.

When he inserted a second finger, the fullness undid me. "Oh my God," I said again, thrusting harder, the music picking up tempo as the pressure building inside me did too. "I'm going to come," I whispered.

"Come." Jake was begging. "God, please come."

And then I did, hard, on his hand, his fingers inside me, the knowledge of that—of *Jake's* fingers inside me, making the orgasm explode and then die down for a moment before cresting again.

My inhibition vanished, and though I stayed quiet, I thrashed and bucked on the bed, letting each wave carry me away. I bit my lip to stifle my cry as I rocked.

Finally, my vision sparkled back as I rode out the last ripples of my orgasm. Jake pulled me tight to him then, to his chest—an embrace both protective and vulnerable, and I relaxed into him. He felt so much like home.

As my breathing returned to a normal pace, a thought bit through my lazy contentment. I'd been selfish. How had I let myself be so selfish with Jake again, right as we'd found each other?

"You should come." I lifted my head from where it had lolled back onto the bed. "Sorry, I..."

"I did. I already came," Jake smiled, a little sheepishly. "Feeling you tighten around my hand, hearing you come. I don't remember that happening on the roof."

I laughed. "We didn't know what we were doing back then. Next time," I promised. "Next time, I want to—"

Jake cut me off. "All I need to hear. I want to know there's a next time."

"There's a next time." I rolled to my side, resting my ear on his chest. Jake wrapped his arms around me, and we lay there, breathing, until my eyelids grew heavy and I gave in to the pull of sleep.

✷✸✷✸✷

CHAPTER 12: JAKE

To say I was disoriented when I woke in my childhood room with Sailor beside me would be an understatement.

I'd gotten up sometime in the night and cleaned myself up while half-lucid—bunched my boxers into a ball and fished an old pair of plaid pajama pants from my dresser.

But now, fully awake, I was downright bewildered. Discombobulated, even.

Before I could brainstorm additional synonyms, Sailor sniffed and slung a heavy arm across my chest, and I had to suppress a laugh. She was so indelicate, even in sleep, and I loved it. She had thrown herself into messing around last night the same way she threw herself into her drumming, and even now, she was approaching sleep with abandon, un-self-consciously sprawled across most of the small bed, her mouth slightly open. The sight of her mouth brought the night rushing back to me, and I was instantly hard.

This had really happened.

And it had really happened while my mother was in the house. Even with The Specials covering any audible evidence of our pleasure, my mom would still have questions. I hadn't slept here in years, let alone with someone.

That someone being Sailor was enough to fuel my mom's meddling for the next decade. The thought of the smug look waiting for us downstairs made my throat burn with last night's wine.

Sailor rolled over again, into a fetal position, leaving me approximately six inches of space. Curving myself around her as the big spoon, I breathed in the fruity scent of her curls, and any thoughts of regret disappeared. It was worth it. All the nagging in the world was worth it.

Seventeen-year-old Jake would have lost his mind at the idea of Sailor in this bed, and current Jake was not much better off. How many times had I jerked off thinking about Sailor in this exact spot? The reality had been so much better.

Sailor had felt bad for focusing on her own pleasure last night, but I loved that too. I loved her unapologetic quest for what she wanted, in life and in bed. I loved the way she held her breath when she was close. I loved the way she gripped my hair, making sure I was exactly where she wanted me.

Loved. The word repeated in my brain. I really did love her—I always had, even when I'd tried to deny it, but I needed to be careful. I had been here before. Last night had made it clear this was definitely not platonic—the idea of Sailor and I ever being platonic was laughable now—but I still didn't know how she felt, not really.

She'd promised me there would be a next time, and it had reassured me, but now, with the morning light shining through the dusty blinds, I realized her promise wasn't enough. I needed to know I wasn't another way for her to cling to the past—some nostalgic balm for the wound Roger was leaving.

Sailor stirred in my arms and my hard on, which had weakened with my worries, returned in full force, pressing against her thighs.

"Well, hello," Sailor said, then yawned as she twisted her torso to face me.

"Hi." I kissed her nose. I wanted to remember this—it was the opposite of waking up from a good dream, with the disappointment of reality washing over you. This was waking up *to* one, the truth of the situation hitting me in wave after wave of gratitude.

She smiled lazily and untwisted, returning to her curled posture, while I took the opportunity to smell her curls again.

"Are you smelling my hair?" Sailor's sleepy mumble was amused.

"Maybe."

Downstairs, dishes clattered—my mom making breakfast.

I sat up and reached for my phone. "Should we call Jerome?" The startled, sleepy confusion in Sailor's eyes as she rolled over to look at me made me want to forget the fear of my mother and curl myself around her again. Almost. "I think my mom's awake."

"I'll call." Sailor blinked as she squirmed up to a seated position and smoothed her clothes from the night before. "I need to pick up some slack."

I couldn't help the smile pulling at my lips as she took the phone from my hands, opened the camp's website again, and put the call on speaker. It only rang once before a deep voice answered. "Jerome Higgins."

"Hi, um…Jerome?" Sailor squeezed her eyes shut and opened them wide, waking herself up. Adorable creases lined her cheek and forehead where the sheets had pressed into them.

"Yes, this is Jerome."

Sailor closed her eyes, softly this time. "I used to be in a ska band—we played with you once at The Barn in Riverside, California."

Immediately, the voice turned jovial. "Oh boy, I remember that show! How'd you find me? Wow, it's been forever since I've heard anyone even say the word 'ska.'"

Sailor flushed, and I knew the memory of the night was as painful for her as it was for me.

"Ah, our trombonist has an incredible memory." Now it was my turn to redden.

"I'll say. Didn't know I was deep in someone's brain like that. Hilarious. How are you kids? Guess you aren't kids anymore, are you? Damn!"

Sailor laughed, and the relief I felt at her mood shift was palpable. So many songs talked about smiles lighting a room. I used to think the image was cliche, but now I knew it was cliche for a reason. Sailor's smile could light an entire block.

"Yeah, not anymore. Oh, congratulations on your camp!"

"Thank you so much. Really, it's an honor to do this work."

Sailor paused. "Yeah, so…we were wondering if you knew where we could find a copy of *Happy Skalidays*. It disappeared from…everywhere, and we really wanted to listen to it."

"Oh, wow. Talk about forever ago." Jerome sounded sentimental. "I don't have copies anymore. My wife was sick of boxes of records cluttering up the house, so I moved them out to the garage, and then I went out there one day and realized they'd all melted."

Sailor's shoulders slumped and I nudged her with my own. After all these years, her disappointment still killed me.

"I think Jimmy has all the digital files. I keep meaning to get ahold of him one of these days, but I haven't gotten around to it." Jerome went on. "We drifted apart after that tour, unfortunately. You know how things get awkward. Then the more time you let go by, the weirder it seems to reach out."

I knew.

But Jerome had said he'd been meaning to get in touch with his former bandmate. So did he…? I cut in. "Do you know *how* to get in touch with him? With Jimmy? We'll ask him and then tell you what we find."

"And who's this?" Jerome's voice was amused.

"Sorry," I said. "I'm the trombonist. Jake."

"Sure, Jake. How could I say no to someone who remembers my fifteen minutes of fame? Let me find you his number."

Briefly, I wondered if my memory might be an advantage for someone applying for the legal researcher position, too. There was a sound like papers rustling, and Sailor and I sat silently, staring at each other. Sailor stuck out her tongue and I had to press my lips together to fight a laugh.

I crossed my eyes in retribution, and Sailor clapped a hand over her mouth. Finally, Jerome came back on the line and gave us the number, and the laugh I'd held in escaped in a hysterical burst. We might actually find this thing.

"Thanks, man." I couldn't help but gush. "Thanks a lot. You have no idea how much this means to us." He really didn't.

When Sailor hung up, there was only a moment of silence before she grabbed my head and wove her fingers through my curls. I clung to her sides as her ribs expanded and contracted under my fingers. We just sat there at first, breathing and grinning, until I couldn't take it. I pressed my lips to Sailor's, and the feel of her heartbeat in my palms made my own dance like Pop Rocks.

We were on a mission now, and the closer we got to completing it, the closer Sailor would get to me. I could be cautious and hopeful at the same time, right? It was hard to worry with her body in my hands, her heart still pounding under my fingers. Kissing Sailor, it was hard to feel anything but a calm certainty this was exactly where we were meant to be.

I couldn't help it. My fingers inched upward. They were almost to her armpits when I noticed. "Oh, shit." I pulled away from the kiss, patting the sides of her like a TSA agent. "You took your bra off. Wasn't expecting that. That's an interesting development. I am totally, casually interested in that fact and not at all fighting a giant boner right now."

She laughed, but pulled away and thrusted the phone back toward me. "You do it."

I ignored the flash of doubt. She definitely wasn't regretting hooking up. Or already annoyed with me. Or...or...I don't know. She just wanted to find the record. "Ok." I took a deep breath. "I will just put this thing right..." I squirmed and tucked myself under the waistband of my pajama pants. "Here." I took the phone from Sailor's hand. "Your magnanimity's reached its limits?"

"Hey, I hate phone calls, too. But I still owe you a non-self imposed orgasm."

"I'll add it to your tab," I said, deadpan, opening my notes app and typing "orgasm" before Sailor smacked my shoulder and clicked on the phone icon. We squeezed each other's hands as the phone rang…and rang…and rang. Our grips slackened as it rang some more. Finally, it went to voicemail.

"You've reached Jimmy Danger. Leave me a message if you want to." Sailor drummed the fingers of her free hand on her lap.

"Yeah, um," I started, after the beep. "This is Jake. I played trombone in a ska band. We played together once in Riverside. Hopefully you can give me a call back." Sailor dropped my hand as I hung up.

"It's ok. He'll call back and if he doesn't, we'll—"

Sailor ignored my reassurances, and cut me off. "It's weird he says 'Jimmy Danger' in his voicemail message, right? When Jerome seemed like they hadn't played together in ages?"

"Yeah, that's pretty weird," I agreed.

But before we could say more, the phone lit up on my lap. We sat up straighter and grabbed hands again. Oh, shit. It was him.

CHAPTER 13: SAILOR

"Hello?" Jake and I locked eyes as we answered in unison. He pressed the button to put it on speaker.

"Jimmy Danger here."

"Jimmy, yeah, we…" Jake started.

Jimmy interrupted. "What band were you in?"

"Skankin' Kiddos. We played with you in—"

"Riverside. I remember." I winced—of course he remembered. I stared at the phone and fought the urge to hang up, but Jake reached out to rub my arm, and the reminder that the scene I'd made hadn't been the end to our story helped ease the feelings which had festered for the last decade.

"What can I do for you? You have another gig for me?"

"Sorry, no gigs." Jake flashed me a bemused look. "We haven't played together in awhile. We were actually wondering if you could tell us where to get a copy of *Happy Skalidays*."

"Ah, yeah. I took them down. Those big fucking companies streaming my music for free and making a killing. Fuck that. I gave the physical copies to Jerry. Figured he could keep everything in that big house of his."

A sense of dread landed like an anvil in my stomach.

Jake and I looked at each other, alarmed. "You gave all of them to Jerry?" I asked.

Jimmy didn't answer. Instead, he chuckled. "Hey, you were hot. Are you still hot?"

I blinked.

Jake grabbed the phone. "You gave all the records to Jerry? And you don't have any CDs or anything?" The anger in his voice and the protectiveness it gave away made me forget my shock and embarrassment for a moment. He kept his eyes locked on mine, wide.

"CDs always sold out at shows. We couldn't keep 'em in stock. They were just burnt things anyway."

"Who kept your music files?" Jake asked.

"That would be me," Jimmy said.

"Well, where are they?" He shook his head slowly and mouthed, "This dude."

"Who fucking knows? Probably a hard drive somewhere. Why does it matter? A lot of good the band did me anyway."

Jake's shoulders sagged. It was my turn to give a reassuring arm rub, and he leaned his head on mine in answer. "Ok. Thanks. Hey, if you happen to come across the album, can you give me a call?"

"I'll do that right after the big ska revival." Jimmy's voice was dripping with sarcasm.

"Thanks, man." I wasn't sure if I had ever heard Jake so annoyed. He ended the call.

"Well, shit," I said.

"Yeah. Shit."

"That was weird," I said.

"Guy's a dick, and totally stuck in the past."

My jaw tensed. "I guess." What did Jake mean "stuck in the past"? Did he think I was stuck in the past, too? Weren't we both on a scavenger hunt for a record from ten years ago? If being stuck in the past was so bad, what was he doing here with me at all?

The edges of Jake's ears turned red as he tried to backpedal. "I mean, he said the thing about the big house. Is he still living in the apartment where they took all their album photos?"

"I don't know." I still lived in the place Roger and I had lived since graduation. "Would that really be so sad?"

My mom had been so fickle while I was growing up. She'd stayed in the same house, sure, but sometimes it had felt like I had a new mother each year. I never knew what she would be in to next. I suddenly realized staying put wasn't only about Rainbow's neediness. It also gave me some constancy—a sense of control.

The phone rang before Jake could answer me. "Hello?" He squeezed my shoulder and attempted an apologetic smile, but I still couldn't meet his eyes.

"Hey, yeah, uh. It's Danger again" I looked up, snapped out of my brooding by the possibility of triumph, and leaned closer to hear. "I'll get you kids the music."

"Oh man, thanks." I knew Jake's relief was partly about Jimmy saving him from our conversation. "We really appreciate it, you don't know how much it—"

"But," Jimmy cut him off. "You have to find me a gig. A good one."

"I don't know how we're supposed to—"

I grabbed the phone from Jake. "We'll do it."

An idea was already forming in my head. We knew Elgin now. He would totally hook us up. I knew for a fact he was nostalgic for the shows The Barn used to host. Maybe Danger would let me play with him. I couldn't ignore the tingling in my fingers when I thought about the possibility of playing a real gig, myself.

"We'll do it at The Barn. When can you come out?"

"That's the thing, babe. You'll need a plan. I don't fly."

"How the fuck are we supposed to book you a gig in New York?" I turned to Jake, whose face was now a bright red as he spoke.

"You don't fly?" I asked.

"Nope. Fucking terrified. The tour bus days were good to me. The last time I flew, Jerry and Tony had to hold both my hands. Tried to punch the stewardess cause she wouldn't let me off the plane."

"We'll come get you." The words were out of my mouth before I could think them through. "We'll hold your hands."

I'd been concerned about my account balance when I bought Jake a burger...now I was offering multiple plane tickets? I closed my eyes and pinched the bridge of my nose.

Jake took the phone from my other hand as Jimmy spoke again. "You kids are going to fly to New York and put me on a plane to California?" I couldn't tell if he was ecstatic or incredulous. The idea really was absurd, even aside from the money aspect.

Jake answered this time. "Yup."

Welp, there was no turning back now. As if he knew I was reconsidering, Jake turned to me and shrugged. "I have a couple thousand dollars put away."

"It's a lot of money though...round trip for us and him and...shit."

"What?"

"Would we have to go twice? To get him back to New York?"

"Isn't Roger going to New York soon?"

I froze. Jake knew about Roger leaving. Of course he did. Hillary had told him all about it. She had probably been thrilled. And Jake...Jake had probably pitied me. He really did think I was a child—broke and alone, too immature to get a real job like he had.

"Oh....uh, yeah, right. He can fly back with Roger."

"When were you born?" Jake knew perfectly well how old I was. Was he being patronizing—confirming my pessimistic fears by pointing out how old we were and how little I had done with my life? I tried to swallow, but my mouth was dry.

"February 1, 1986," Jimmy said.

Jake opened the notes app and typed in the date, right under "orgasm." The joke from less than an hour ago felt stale now.

Oh. Right. We would need his birthday for the plane ticket.

I let out a breath. I was overreacting—seeing things in Jake's words that weren't there. Like always, I was convinced everyone was looking down on me and judging me. Also...Jimmy Danger was only like ten years older than us? The gap had seemed a lifetime when we were teenagers. Even now, he seemed so old and jaded.

"Got it. Thanks, man. We'll be in touch soon."

Jake looked at me after hanging up, barely containing his smile.

"I really can't afford to help much with the plane tickets." I hated to dampen the mood again.

Jake shook his head. "No worries. I'll get them."

"No," I said firmly. "You should go alone." I was not about to put myself in that position. Even if Jake hadn't intended to belittle me, I wasn't going to give him a reason to do so.

"No way."

"I don't want to owe you money *and* an orgasm."

He actually laughed.

"What?"

Jake shook his head. "Nothing."

"What?" I pressed.

"The idea of you owing me anything." Jake laughed again, but I still didn't get what was so funny.

"Sailor," he said. "I owe you everything. As kids...now. You're constantly saving me from being a shitty version of myself. If this is what it takes to show you what you mean to me, I could care less about my savings account."

I softened. "Jake." The gesture still seemed extreme, but he was so sweet. He had always been able to open up—to say mushy things without seeming mushy—to make *me* feel mushy despite my best efforts. "It's a lot of money."

"Well, I'm not flying Jimmy Danger out here alone."

I laughed now, though I knew he wasn't joking—Danger had genuinely irked him.

"Fine. But I don't owe you."

"You don't owe me." Jake crossed his heart, his face so earnest, I couldn't help but smirk.

"Just a hand job," I said.

Jake's eyes widened and his face turned so red I thought he might combust.

"I'm kidding! Chill!"

Jake exhaled a laugh. "I mean, if you're offering..."

I shoved him on the shoulder.

"I'm kidding," he said. "Let's order tickets."

Five minutes later, Jake put down the phone. "Done," he said. "We're going to New York."

"We're going to New York," I said, hardly able to believe it.

"We're going to New York!" Jake repeated. It took another minute for the reality to hit me, and apparently Jake took as long to process. Suddenly, he turned and pulled me into a hug.

"We're going to New York!" I squealed into his shoulder.

"Soon!" Jake said.

"Soon!" I pulled away and we stared at each other in disbelief.

"We should visit the old CBGB site," Jake said. "And Arlene's Grocery."

"Are there other legendary ska sites?" This was really real. I was starting to get excited.

"I'm sure we could ask Danger," Jake said. "He's totally hung up on his old ska days."

I froze. This was the second jab Jake had made that was as applicable to me as to Jimmy Danger. "I would love to play ska again."

"That's not what I meant." Jake rubbed the back of his neck. "He's like...sad." He was panicking, turning red, trying to save face. But I couldn't let it go.

I crossed my arms. "How do you know I'm not sad?"

"Because you could get a different job if you wanted. You have a degree." He licked his lips. "I thought you liked teaching drum lessons." Something about the way he said it made me feel like a child.

Like someone had flipped a switch, all the energy building in my body as excitement tumbled out as shaky fury. He had been judging me. He pitied me. He thought I was a fool. I'd pushed down my insecurity about being broke, but now it bubbled up. But fuck that. Jake was right. I *could* have a better paying job, and there were reasons I'd chosen not to. "I mean, I don't love it all the time, but I also don't want to sell out to some corporate gig." I stood.

"What's that supposed to mean?" Jake stood now too, his voice hard.

Apparently we hadn't resolved anything in the last ten years. If we didn't hash it out now, it would fester until we did.

"I think you know what I mean. Paralegal? That's not you, Jake. You had an anarchy symbol scrawled on your backpack in Sharpie"

"How do you know what's me?" Jake shook his head. "You haven't talked to me in ten years. Maybe I enjoy being a paralegal."

Maybe Jake really had changed in the last ten years, but I hadn't thought it possible to change this much. "Really? Really, you enjoy being a paralegal?" I couldn't help the acidity.

"Maybe I enjoy being a responsible adult. Maybe I enjoy growing up."

Oof. I actually felt the words in my gut. "And what's *that* supposed to mean? I haven't grown up?"

"Have you? Isn't that why it's so painful Roger's leaving? Because he was the last person who enabled your childishness?"

Angry tears stung my eyes. He didn't know about the nights I stayed up late, worrying if I was doing enough for my drum students, or the mornings I rose at 5am to work the breakfast shift at the diner. He had no idea what it felt like to stand on your feet for eight hours or wait on a rude Sunday church crowd you knew would leave an abysmal tip.

"I don't have to listen to this. Maybe I don't want to grow up if it means betraying who I am. Maybe I'm more like Jimmy Danger than you think. Maybe I like who I am."

Jake hung his head and blew out a slow breath, then looked back up at me. "Maybe I like who I am, too."

I didn't know what to say. I also liked who Jake was. Deep down, he was always Jake, no matter what he did for a job, no matter how boring a house he lived in.

But his feelings for me were conditional, like they always had been. We wouldn't work now for the same reason we hadn't worked when we were seventeen. Jake couldn't get rid of the external pressure to be something he wasn't, and I wasn't willing to compromise.

Jake went on. "You jumped on the chance to get Danger a gig because you're still clinging to old dreams too. It has nothing to do with the album or with me, does it?"

"Are you saying I did something for myself? Forgive me! Isn't that why you went to Berkeley? Haven't we established we don't owe each other anything?"

Now Jake was silent.

"I should go." I wanted him to stop me, to say my name, to call me back, but he didn't. Just like at The Barn.

He stood, arms crossed, in his bedroom. Ten years ago, before we'd taken each other's virginities on the roof of a gas station across from our high school, I'd imagined it happening here. Now it all felt like a mistake.

I shook my head and thumped down the stairs. I dreaded running into Mrs. Rosenblatt. How would I explain my presence here? And my forthcoming absence? I couldn't fake a smile and hug right now.

Thankfully, I made it out the door without any contact. Outside, the sun mocked me, shining bright enough I had to squint, as if daring me to admit I didn't love its year-round burn.

As I drove home, I blasted Less Than Jake's "Ghosts of You and Me," the sound roaring out of the car window and into the bright winter day.

I shouted the lyrics, feeling the lines about heartbreak in my bones. I was dizzy before I realized how hard I was singing along.

Back in my room at home, I looked at the photos I'd stuck to my wall years before. I could move into the master suite now. At least there was that. My own room was small, meant for a child—fair, since Roger paid so much of the rent. I'd painted the walls in a checker block pattern and pasted pictures of fashion inspiration—mod women with bob haircuts, rude girls with shaved heads, all of them looking bored and indifferent—like nothing as insignificant as love could get under their skin.

I began to pick at one of the photos. It was Pauline Black, her gender ambiguous, her face bored and angry. What courage it must have taken to be an androgynous Black ska weirdo back in her day. I wished I could summon even a little bit of her bravery.

I looked into Pauline's eyes and tried to absorb her boldness, praying to her as if she were the patron saint of rude girls. There was no divine revelation, no granting of grace.

It was all bullshit. Ska hadn't saved me from anything. Fuck ska. All it had done was make me an outcast and keep me from other people. It had allowed me to build a wall around myself.

I thought it would protect me, but really it had kept me alone.

The build ups and let downs of the last couple days were too much. My adrenaline was depleted, and I felt like I could nap until the New Year.

Slipping my fingernail further under the corner of the photo, I peeled it from the wall and watched as it fluttered to the floor.

APRIL 11, 2013

JakeTheB@ndG33k: Have you gotten any college letters yet?

xDrummerChickx: Nah. I'm gonna go to Chaffey CC

JakeTheB@ndG33k: Wait, you didn't even apply anywhere else?

xDrummerChickx: I can't really afford it and I like it here anyway. Plus my mom and the band and stuff.

JakeTheB@ndG33k: I was thinking we might go together

xDrummerChickx: go where? Where did you apply?

JakeTheB@ndG33k: UC Riverside…

xDrummerChickx: Riverside isn't far!

JakeTheB@ndG33k: as a safety…I'm kind of hoping for Berkeley

xDrummerChickx: oh

JakeTheB@ndG33k: you could apply to a cc up there!

xDrummerChickx: yeah maybe…

CHAPTER 14: SAILOR

"Excuse me. What did you do to Pauline?" I looked up from where I'd been sitting with my head in my hands for the last hour, and saw Roger in my doorway with his hands on his hips, staring at the shredded photo on the floor. His face softened as he saw mine.

"Honey, what's wrong?" he asked, and the tears I'd been holding back came rushing out like the glacier of my heart had melted and the remains of the polar ice caps were pouring from my eyes.

"I'm so sorry I was such a bitch to you."

"You know we don't use that word in this house unless we're talking about a Republican."

I laughed through snotty tears as Roger stepped into my room to perch beside me on the bed. He rested his hands on his knees, ready to spring up if necessary. I hated how I'd put him on alert like that—like I might attack him again.

"But I was awful. I'm so sorry. I want you to go where you'll be happy. I'll just miss you."

"I know." Roger pulled me in for a hug. I squeezed my eyes shut as I rested my chin on his shoulder and felt his body relax. "That's why I was planning to make peace until I saw what you did to your room. I'll miss you, too. So much." He leaned back and took both my hands. "Now tell me what's wrong."

I spilled the whole story, from calling Jimmy Danger to buying tickets to New York, replaying every word Jake and I had said.

When I was done, Roger kissed me on the forehead. "I'm so proud of you."

"What? Why? You were right. You told me this was a terrible idea."

"Of course I was right." Roger smirked. "But you were brave. It was brave to go after him, and it was brave to walk away. I wish I were as brave as you."

I scoffed, but Roger's face remained earnest.

"I'm serious. It's why I'm going back to New York."

"What do you mean?"

"Sailor, you have been unapologetically you since the day we met. It took me ten years to absorb enough of your courage to go back and face the city, let alone my family. Whenever I start to worry about seeing my mom again or trying to make it on my own there, I tell myself to channel you. You're my idol." A smile pulled at one side of Roger's mouth as his eyes darted to the picture on the floor. "Scratch that. Pauline is my idol. But you're a close second, so I guess I can forgive your blasphemy."

My laugh was watery but genuine. For years, Roger's financial support had made me feel infantile. I'd hated relying on him as much as I'd needed to. But this new revelation made me think maybe our relationship hadn't been as unequal as I'd thought. Maybe Roger didn't pity me. The possibility made new tears spring to my eyes. "You're going to do amazing. I don't think you're capable of any less."

"I am not." The usual sparkle was returning to his irises. "Now, come help me pack."

I followed my friend out to the living room where he plopped to the floor and began folding a leopard print silk shirt. Clothes, books, and open luggage lay all around him. Apparently I had stumbled by the whole mess in my huff, but now that my head was clear, the poignancy was impossible to ignore.

"It's really happening, huh?" I stood before it all and looked at the shirts and jackets, while I tried not to remember where he had worn each one.

Roger picked up a Reel Big Fish t-shirt which he had somehow kept in mint condition. He'd worn it to our celebratory dinner the night his little brother had graduated from college across the country. He'd been so proud of Jerrick and so sad to be so far away. I'd taken him to Indian and he'd panicked when korma dripped on the collar, but the stain remover in his bag had done its job.

Now, Desmond, who had been resting with legs against the wall, scrambled to her feet, and trotted over to sit in Roger's lap, stepping on clothing and books in the process. Roger lifted the Reel Big Fish shirt over the dog's head, so it blocked his own face, and continued to fold.

I took the opportunity to really look at what I could see of my best friend. For the first time, I saw how vulnerable he really was—how much courage this move required—and any remaining resentment dissipated. It wasn't about me—this was what Roger needed to do, and I felt happy and hopeful for him despite knowing I would miss him terribly.

Roger finished folding the tee, tucked it into a blue suitcase, and looked up at me. "It's really happening." We were quiet for a long moment. Finally, Roger leapt back to his feet. "Let's light the candles."

"The Hannukah candles? It's 10 a.m."

Roger waved the comment away. "It's five o'clock somewhere."

At my suspicious smirk, he continued. "I'm going to the Temple later. But we haven't celebrated together this year and I don't want to miss it." He didn't have to say why. Our time together was precious, because it was limited.

"You've packed two shirts."

Roger looked down at the chaos at his feet and shrugged. "I'll do more later."

"I don't have a menorah."

"I have one." He turned on his heel and headed for the kitchen. I followed, watching as he reached up to a high cabinet.

"I love that you have a menorah," I said as he set it on the counter separating the kitchen from the living room, opened the junk drawer, and from amidst Sierra Club address labels, loose coins, and dried up pens, pulled out an old box of matches and some linty multicolored Hanukkah candles. Sorting through and tossing out broken ones, he selected four and slotted them into their respective spots.

"Of course I have a menorah. Roger smiled as he extended the hand with the matches my way.

I shook my head. "Please, you do it....I'm sorry I said the Jewish stuff was weird."

Roger shrugged. "It is kind of weird. I never minded being weird."

"Really. It was fucked up to gatekeep. There's nothing about being Black or gay that means you can't be Jewish. And you don't have to be Jewish to go to Temple."

"I know."

Understanding dawned. "That's why you go."

Roger smiled. "Part of it."

"But you were right about me."

"About ska?" Roger sighed. "Is that why you took down Pauline?"

"No. That was about Jake."

"Ah." Roger nodded thoughtfully. "Well, I think it's ok you love ska."

"But you were right. It's appropriative."

"I can't speak for every Black person—"

"Obviously."

"Obviously." He leaned an elbow on the counter as his brow creased in consideration. "But I think the shitty kind of appropriation is usually about taking blindly or taking without acknowledgement or taking without repayment. You know ska started with Black people and you honor it. You don't consume the music and then go vote against Black interests."

I nodded, still not entirely sure.

"I think we misfits have to find home where we can. Come here." Roger pulled me into a hug. "And as long as we're not assholes, and we give back to the community, maybe a little appropriation is acceptable."

I shouldn't have been surprised Roger knew the Hebrew prayer or that he said it with such conviction. After, we stared at the firelight for several breaths until eventually, Roger sighed, and the flames flickered in his exhale.

I followed him over to the table, both of us walking toe-heel, neither wanting to disturb the hush now filling the house.

"What if Jake is right?" I asked, finally. "What if I need to grow up?"

Roger pursed his lips and sighed. "Do you think he's right?"

"Maybe," I admitted. I didn't want to be a paralegal, but I didn't want to be...this, either. Maybe Jake's comments had hurt so much because they were too close to my own deprecating self-talk.

"Then maybe it's time for a little reflection. But right or not, no one treats my best friend that way." He kissed me on the forehead again. "Now...I have to take Desmond out. Get as many walks as we can in before she's stuck in a New York apartment."

I nodded. I didn't deserve my best friend. "Thank you," I said.

"Always." He booped my nose for good measure and called to his dog. From the counter, the candles glittered as they melted, rainbow wax forming shiny puddles on the granite.

CHAPTER 15: JAKE

I sat on my bed with my head in my hands for a long time. How could my emotions swing so wildly over the course of a single day?

In the past 24 hours I had been nervous, excited, relieved, horny as hell, happier than I'd ever been, nostalgic, pissed, and now...what was I now? Now, I was confused.

What had Sailor and I even fought about? How had it even started? And why was I more shaken up about this than about my years-long relationship ending? I knew the answer to that one at least.

I loved Sailor. I had always loved Sailor, and I would always love Sailor. Maybe she was right about my deeper feelings. Did part of me look down on her for refusing to grow up? And could I live with her disappointment at my own compromises?

"I forgot to mention last night, there are some things to go through in your room before I donate it all."

I jumped at my mom's voice in the doorway. "Jesus fucking Christ, Ma."

"The one on Haven has such a strange system—you know they sort all the shirts by color instead of style? Who do you know who shops by color? Although, I guess it is good for people who need a certain color for a uniform. I always like how some stores put all their employees in red. It makes them easier to find. Though, once I asked a young lady where to find the seasonal tumblers and she looked at me like I had an extra head. It took me a minute to realize she was a shopper and just happened to be wearing red! Whenever I go there now, I make sure I'm not wearing red." She let out a loud chortle.

When I stared back blankly, my mom cleared her throat and rearranged her expression as if she'd remembered I was her son and not a gab buddy from the Temple Sisterhood.

"Anyway, I sorted through a lot, but there's still a bunch in the closet. I didn't want to bother you while Sailor was still here, but—"

"Thanks, Ma."

"Where did Sailor head off to so early anyway? She should have stayed for breakfast, at least. I would have made French toast."

I ignored the question. I was not in the mood to discuss my overnight guest. "I'll sort through the stuff."

For once, my mom took the hint.

It took a good five minutes after she left to drag myself from my spot on the bed.

Finally, I crossed the room to the closet, knelt before the open door, and began to dig through the contents with shaking hands. I flipped pages of photo albums filled with snapshots from band field trips, avoiding the album Sailor had made me for Valentine's Day our senior year.

My fingers found the yarmulka-clad teddy bear from my Bar Mitzvah and an alien I'd won at Ring Toss at the Lemon Festival in sixth grade. Finally, they brushed against something hard and textured that was wedged behind a box and the wall. I knew the shape instantly.

Carefully, I removed the dusty case from the back of the closet and lay it open before me. "Hey, buddy," I muttered, as I lifted the instrument and inserted the slide into its brass body.

Unlike my own softer, hairier self, the physical shape of my trombone was completely unchanged. My hands knew each curve as I brought the mouthpiece to my lips and blew. It was honky at first, dust puffing out from the bell, but soon the sound grew clearer and fuller, my arm moving the slide from muscle memory.

My mouth and nose protested, still sore from their collision. I hadn't even noticed the pain when Sailor and I were kissing. I could only play for a moment before my lungs also wanted me to fuck off. I hadn't realized as a kid how much breath control playing took. I hadn't appreciated being young enough.

I set the instrument down and went back to the closet for the last photo album. There, on the front page, was a picture of me and Sailor, seventeen years old, grins plastered across our faces along with our sweaty hair, band helmets tucked under our arms. On the next page was a candid shot I'd taken of her at a Skankin' Kiddos practice, sitting behind her drum set, sticking out her tongue at someone outside the frame.

Page after page, I looked at grainy snapshots and Polaroids covered with hearts and stars doodled by Sailor.

As a kid, you don't realize how much stupid jokes and goofy grins will mean later.

And then, as if the fist squeezing my lungs wasn't making it hard enough to breathe, folded between the last two pages was the flyer—the flyer from our first and only show that had stopped me in my tracks when I'd seen it on the door of The Barn. I had put it in my pocket when we'd arrived at the venue, thinking it would be a sweet souvenir—a reminder of the best night of my life to date. I'd gotten home that night and stuffed the flyer into the photo album, unable to bring myself to trash it. I hadn't seen it since.

This could have been a moment of redemption. Sailor could have been here with me, and we could have rediscovered this together. I felt sick imagining it—thinking about how much I wanted that instead of...this.

God, I was an asshole. The photos, my trombone, the flyer—I'd forgotten until I saw them all again how that time felt in my gut. But Sailor had remembered—had felt how important it was back then, too, even without nostalgia, and she'd tried to tell me. Twice.

I wanted to call, but there was no way she wanted to talk to me. I'd made it crystal clear I was a dick, and if I wanted to prove otherwise, I would have to do better than a phone call. I would have to show her how much she meant to me—how much music meant to me, especially the music we made together.

Suddenly, my spine straightened. *Show* her. That was it—a show. It was the perfect grand gesture. Maybe goofy romcoms hadn't failed me after all.

But would Sailor still go to New York with me? There was no way I was going to New York to get Jimmy Danger alone. Somehow I would convince her. Maybe the trip would be enough—all those ska landmarks, a change of scenery. But then when we got back, I would surprise her with our old bandmates and really seal the deal. We could play one last song— one last hurrah before Roger left— and fix the bad memories she associated with The Barn, and with me.

We could change our story.

I would have to get the rest of the band on board. Not Hillary, obviously, but the rest of them. And we'd have to practice, I realized, as I thought about the pain in my chest—the one I couldn't blame on heartache. I had to rebuild my playing stamina.

I knew Sonia still lived in Upland, working as a hygienist at my dentist's office, because I saw her there every six months or so, though at my most recent cleaning, I'd specifically asked the woman at the front desk not to have her. It was too weird having someone I knew look at my teeth.

I hadn't seen Romero in years, but I knew he was working at a warehouse a town over. Steady, chill, just like always. Go, too, had stuck around and become a car salesman for a local dealership. It wasn't something I would have predicted, but in hindsight, with his enthusiastic, slightly vulgar attitude, it made perfect sense.

Everyone's adult selves made perfect sense, actually—like they had materialized into the best possible versions of what they were meant to become.

Except for me—I'd gotten off course somehow. Well, now was the time to get back on track.

Once everyone confirmed, I would call Elgin, make flyers, post on social media. Or maybe not on social media—it would be too hard to keep it from both Hillary and Sailor. As it was, the hard part would be getting Sailor to a practice, let alone to New York. I needed Roger in my corner. With the photo album in one hand and my trombone in the other, I went downstairs, propelled by new purpose.

"Bye, Ma."

She turned from where she sat at the dining room table, where the night before, the atmosphere had seemed auspicious. Now that she had cleared the plates and the menorah sat in its usual place above the fireplace, it was like our celebration had never happened.

"This is all you're keeping?" She eyed my spoils.

I nodded. "It's all I need."

"Oh, Jake. I forgot to ask."

I stopped in my tracks and adjusted the grip on my trombone. "Yeah?"

"What are all these charges on your credit card lately? I saw airline tickets? Is that for work? They should really be paying for those. Or do they reimburse you later?"

What the *fuck?* "How are you seeing my credit card charges?"

"Well, you know I had to co-sign for your card in college. I just like to keep up with it. It's so easy to get in over your head. It's no problem at all. I just click over on the little tab when I'm checking mine and—"

"Ma. I am almost thirty. I do not need you checking my financial records."

"I know you don't *need* me to, but—."

"I don't *want* you to. I'm calling the bank later and taking you off. Jesus." I shook my head. I needed to get out of this house. How else had my mom and Hillary been treating me like a child? This whole grownup thing I felt so proud of was all an act.

Mom pretended to examine her long red nails. "So, the airline tickets?"

"It's none of your business, Ma." I turned and walked out the door before she could scold me.

Back at my house, I perched on the edge of the couch, elbows leaning on knees, and scrolled through my contacts until I found Roger's number. I was almost sure he would be up for it. He, like me, would do anything for Sailor—as long as he wasn't too pissed to talk to me.

I hit call and held my breath as it rang.

We'd ignored each other at every fundraiser and school concert, my pile of shitty moves—leaving Sailor, leaving the band, dating Hillary—wedged between us like a musical rest—only more apparent because of its silence. Roger had been like a brother to me once.

At those school events, I made a point not to look at Roger as he introduced his students, studying the program or the hair of the person in front of me or the position of the stage lights, and Roger, like he knew exactly where I was seated, always projected his speech to the opposite side of the room. I knew Sailor attended those events too, and I knew in reality, he was probably speaking in her direction, but I'd made an effort to block her presence there from my mind.

What had Sailor told him? There was no doubt he would be furious if she'd filled him in. Hopefully he'd forgive me when he learned what I was planning.

Roger answered after three rings. "Yes?" His voice was muffled by outside sounds—cars zipping by, wind, birds singing late-morning songs.

"Hi...I...." I started. A car horn blared on Roger's end. "I wanted to talk to you about something," I blurted.

"Sorry." Roger's tone was dry. "I can't hear you."

"Wait!" I shouted. I couldn't let him blow me off so easily.

Roger was quiet, but he didn't hang up. There was no question he had talked to Sailor.

"I want to fix it. And I have an idea."

"Go on." He sounded skeptical. I explained my plans for the trip, for getting the band back together for one last song.

"You think Sailor will go to New York with you? After you confirmed the thing she's worried about for ten years?"

"Wait, what? What did I confirm?"

"You know, your mom likes to brag about you at Temple, but I don't think you're as smart as she says you are. You're definitely not as handsome."

It was a low blow, but I deserved it. "I know I made her feel like shit. That's why I want to do this."

Roger scoffed. "'Like shit' is an understatement. You made her feel like shit in high school, and I've been picking up the pieces ever since. I had finally almost convinced her your opinion did not define her, that she could follow her dreams and fulfill her obligations, and then you go and show up. Not even a fucking week and you're in her head again. She literally ripped the ska photos off her wall today, right as I'm about to leave. I'm a fucking mess thanks to you, and I've been doing my best to put on a brave face for her and—"

"I want to make it right. For her and you. Please, man. Give me a chance."

Had Sailor really been hurting this whole time? Roger's accusations made my throat sting. God, I wanted to hold her—to tell her I hadn't meant any of it—then, or now—that I had never stopped wanting her exactly how she is, and I hated the part of me that insisted on making her feel otherwise.

"Well, good luck." Roger's voice was still tinged with sarcasm, but "good luck" was an improvement from the "fuck off" we had essentially started with.

I went on. "I need your help. I know she won't go to New York unless you think it's a good idea."

"I *don't* think it's a good idea."

"I know." I sighed. "Look." Roger wasn't going to make this easy, and I didn't blame him. He had every right to hate me and to be protective of Sailor. But I had to try. "I never stopped loving her. Not for a minute. Not when she stormed out, not when she ignored the messages I tried to send all of freshman year at college, not ever. And whether you help me or not—whether this plan works or not—I never will stop loving her. Please. Let me show her. And you. I'll be good to her, I swear it. I won't fuck this up again."

My heart thudded in my ears as I waited for Roger to respond. If it weren't for the constant whoosh of wind I might have worried he'd hung up. When he finally spoke, it was an octave lower than his usual range. "You better not make me regret this."

My limbs went liquid with relief. "Thanks, dude. Seriously. You don't know how much I appreciate it. I won't. I promise I won't."

"You hurt her again and I might literally kill you."

I believed him. "Noted. You have my permission."

Roger was still less than enthusiastic. "I have to get the dog home."

He would see. I would prove myself to everyone. "So you'll play? At The Barn?"

"You get Sailor on board somehow, and I'll play."

My heart was racing—my body and brain eager to get everything in order. "Deal!"

The sound of the wind stopped as soon as Roger ended the call.

April 15, 2013

SaVedNSwEet: hey, you around?

JakeTheB@ndG33k: hey Hill, what's up?

SaVedNSwEet: I'm getting kind of nervous for the show

JakeTheB@ndG33k: you'll do great. Now me? I'm nervous

SaVedNSwEet: thanks…but how come?

JakeTheB@ndG33k: I'm really hoping to make it amazing for Sailor…like a big "goodbye to high school" kind of thing. I've been trying to convince her to come up to Berkeley with me but I think she needs closure, you know?

SaVedNSwEet: oh

JakeTheB@ndG33k: what?

SaVedNSwEet: nothing

JakeTheB@ndG33k: no, what?

SaVedNSwEet: Sailor is just kind of stubborn. I think she's going to do what she wants to do no matter what

JakeTheB@ndG33k: and that's why I need this show to be epic

CHAPTER 16: SAILOR

I could tell something was off as soon as Roger and Desmond walked through the front door. My best friend's usual smile didn't reach his eyes. I tipped my head in question, but before I could ask what was up, Desmond broke the silence with a loud bark that drew my attention from Roger to the dog. My eyes stung. I would miss Desmond too.

"It's going to be a big change for her...the move." I placed my half-eaten peanut butter and banana sandwich on the plate in front of me. I hadn't had an appetite since the fight with Jake, and attempts to force food into my system only made me more depressed. I'd even drizzled the bread in honey, but I could still hardly taste it.

"She's going to hate it." Roger bent to release Desmond from her leash, and the dog dashed to her water dish, where she frantically lapped, splashing more drops of liquid to the floor than she got into her mouth. "She's so used to the yard and the dog park and good weather year round...all the walks."

"I hadn't even thought about the walks. Are you going to put her in little sweaters and boots for her walks in the snow?" The image made me smirk in spite of my misery.

Roger stage sighed. "I never thought I would be that kind of gay. God, I'm not looking forward to snow either. I do look cute in puffer jackets though."

At once, an idea flashed across my mind—a bare lightbulb in an otherwise dark room. I would be by myself soon. Roger was worried about Desmond in New York. Maybe...The thought brought with it the first hint of anything close to happiness I had felt since Jake booked the New York tickets last night.

Wow—how had that only been last night? I felt like the meme from Titanic with the woman saying "It's been 84 years."

Roger took a glass from the cabinet and poured himself some water.

If I kept Desmond, she wouldn't have to adjust to the weather or the lack of space. Roger wouldn't have to worry about her trashing his apartment.

And I wouldn't be entirely alone.

I dismissed the thought quickly. There was no way I could ask something like that of Roger. Desmond was his baby.

Sure, we had gone together to the shelter, and sure, I had taken Desmond for her lunch time walks since she was a roly poly puppy. Sure, she sometimes snuggled at my feet, warming them like the coziest socks, as I sat at my drums with a notepad, writing out cadences and planning lessons.

But she was Roger's dog—that had always been clear. Roger had named her—had settled on Desmond Dekker after the 1960s legend of ska, reggae, and rocksteady. Roger paid for her food and vet bills, and Roger took her to the dog park for several hours every weekend. But Roger was looking from me to Desmond intently. "It's too bad..." He trailed off. "Nevermind."

My chest fluttered. "What?"

"She'd be happier here." Roger paused. "But I could never ask you. You have enough on your plate."

I blinked rapidly. "What if I wanted to keep her?"

"Do you?" Roger sat next to me and placed his water glass on the table. It swirled and reflected our faces in its distorted, shifting surface. I could tell my friend was torn about the prospect. He really loved his dog—enough to want what was best for her. I should give him an out, even if the possibility of keeping Desmond here was easing the weight I'd felt pressing on my shoulders since the fight. I even felt a flicker of hunger in my belly as I caught a whiff of my sandwich.

"You know I love Desmond, but she's your dog." I stared at Roger's water. "And maybe I only like the idea of someone here to keep me company. I don't know if that's selfish. It's not fair for me to steal your dog because Jake is an asshole."

"Maybe Jake isn't a total asshole," Roger muttered, his own eyes moving to the left—his classic tell. He wasn't being honest but I couldn't understand why. Why even comment on Jake?

"Huh?" I asked.

"Nothing."

"You're the one who told me I shouldn't hang out with him. Now you're a fan?"

Roger shook his head quickly, but his eyes darted to the left again. "Never mind." We sat in awkward silence for several minutes.

"You really want me to?" I asked finally. "Keep Desmond? Wouldn't you miss her?"

"Like hell, but you'd both be happier with her here."

He was really offering to let her stay.

Suddenly, I was the one imagining buying clothes for a dog. I would continue the weekly dog park visits and put all her appointments in my calendar. Maybe I would sign up for training. She could use a new leash. Another benefit of the possible arrangement occurred to me. "Plus it means you will have to come visit."

"Yeah, just to see the dog. I'll have to visit all the time." Roger's smile was mischievous.

"Of course. To see the dog." There was a beat. "I'm going to miss you so much," I said.

He brushed the hair out of my eyes. "I'm going to miss you, too."

★ ★ ★ ★ ★ ★ ★

CHAPTER 17: JAKE

Cool air slapped me in the face as I entered the dental office. The woman at the front desk smiled and pulled her cheeks and chin into a perfect heart.

"Checking in?" Her red curls bounced as she hovered her fingers over her keyboard.

"No, I... um...Is Sonia in today?"

"Sure, I can make sure she's your hygienist. She's great, isn't she? What's your name?"

"No, I..." I shoved my hands into the pockets of my cargo pants. "I don't have an appointment."

The receptionist lowered her hands to her lap and looked up from the computer, her smile guarded. "Is she expecting you?"

"No." I hadn't thought this through. While I totally got it—men are creepy—I hadn't anticipated coming across as a stalker.

"Well, I'm afraid I can't let you back if you don't have an appointment."

"Yeah, that totally makes sense." I sighed and turned to head toward the door, then stopped and turned on the heel of my sneaker. "Do you take walk-ins?"

The woman scowled. "For emergencies. Are you a patient here?"

"Yes!" I said, too excitedly. "I'm a patient. I have a toothache." It wasn't a total lie. My mouth had been sore since trying out my trombone.

The woman rolled her eyes. "A bad one," I added, bringing my hand to my jaw for emphasis.

"Let me see what I can do." As she reached for the mouse with her right hand, her left, disappeared into the purse on the desk, presumably searching for pepper spray.

I gave her my name and birthday, and ten minutes later, I was leaning back in a dentist's chair, a paper bib clipped around my neck. A fish tank burbled in the corner, and a TV mounted on the ceiling for horizontal patients played an animated film.

God, what would the co-pay for this be? I had blown most of my savings on New York tickets. My dental insurance covered two cleanings annually, cavity fillings, and not much else. I had to remind myself I didn't actually have a dental emergency. If I needed to, I could skip my next cleaning.

Sonia walked in through the open door, looking happily surprised to see me, though I was sure she'd seen my name on the chart.

"Hey! Jess said you requested me. I thought you didn't want me looking in your mouth anymore."

"No. It's not—" I tried, but she interrupted.

"It's cool. I get it. It's weird. But hey, nice to see you!"

"Actually," I started, but Sonia had already put on goggles and a mask.

"Let's see. You have a toothache?" She lowered the arm of the overhead light to a foot above my face, and I saw a tattoo peeking out from under the sleeve of her scrubs. I wondered what it was and when she had gotten it. Again, I regretted the time I had missed with my friends.

If I had been hanging out with everyone this whole time, maybe the last ten years would have felt less like treading water and more like chilling on a pool raft with a beer in one hand and good music on the deck.

"No. But I didn't know how else to get ahold of you." Sonia paused her busied readying of tools and tilted her head in confusion. Sonia was friendly, but she had always been cautious around people she didn't know. I could almost see her mind working as she considered she might not really know me anymore.

Maybe I was being a creepy dude after all. Maybe we had all drifted too far apart. Maybe we'd missed a big enough part of each other's lives we'd become different people.

"I'm trying to plan a band reunion," I said.

Sonia barked a laugh and lifted the light back to its original position. "Oh shit! I haven't played sax in forever."

I grinned. Our friendship was still right there—like a radio station waiting for us to tune in.

"It's one song," I explained. "I'm doing it for Sailor."

"Wow, you're a regular John Cusack. Or Tom Hanks? Are either of them Jewish?"

I laughed. "I think John Cusack got in trouble for an antisemitic tweet, actually."

"Not John Cusack then! You're a...Zach Braff."

"I think I'm more a Seth Rogan." I laughed. "But does that mean you're in?"

"Of course! I'll get Romero on board and he'll get Go in, too. They'll both be stoked. I can't wait."

I thought about Romero and his quiet smirks—letting me know I was in on the silent judgment he cast on other people. And then Go, whose filthy mouth was the polar opposite of Romero's chill, but whose love for his friends was off the charts.

What fun would I have had with the two of them if I'd made an effort to stay in touch?

"I can't wait either." I swung my legs around the side of the chair, ready to hoist myself up.

Sonia stopped me. "Wait."

I paused, one hand on a bib clip.

"You can't leave. I have to check your teeth."

"I really don't have a toothache." A jolt of pain bolted through my tooth, mocking my lie.

"Yeah, but you're checked in and everything. I can't not do my job."

"Oh, for sure. I guess it would be a bad look for you." I laid back down.

A stuffed monkey with giant white teeth laughed at me from the counter behind Sonia as she lowered the light again. "Open up. Let's see those pearly whites."

I did as I was told and tried not to think about her crystal clear view up my nose.

"Oh shit, Jake."

"Whaaa?" I hated trying to talk with my mouth open.

"You have a loose molar back here but like, gnarly. Have you had any head trauma lately?"

The Barn door didn't count as head trauma, did it? I shrugged.

Sonia leaned in closer and poked around with something silver. "I'm surprised you're not in serious pain. I'm going to get the doctor."

"Wai—" I tried, my worry about outrageous dental bills renewed, but she had already left.

She came back a moment later with a tall woman in a white coat, her blonde hair tied back in a neat bun.

The dentist took a seat on the stool beside me. "I hear you're vying for a visit from the tooth fairy."

I tried to laugh but gleeked instead, saliva shooting out onto my lip from under my tongue. The dentist leaned over me and her brow furrowed as she began poking around at my mouth.

"Yup, that's pretty nasty. But we'll get you fixed up. A splint should do the trick for now, and lucky for you, we have a cancellation at one."

Holy shit. "One? Like one o'clock today?" I had not anticipated fucking dental surgery today. Especially with all the shit I had to get done for my surprise.

"One o'clock today."

As Sonia typed something into the computer, I began mentally planning the next two hours. I could sit in the pavilion downtown to call Elgin, then go to the library to make fliers. I was trying to be more flexible, wasn't I? Less set in my ways? This would be a good start. Time to get flexible, Jake. We were still on, wired mouth and all.

✦ ✦ ✦ ✦ ✦ ✦

CHAPTER 18: SAILOR

Desmond slept with me that night, for the first time ever, like she had understood the plan. It was after midnight when she nosed open my door, waddled over to my bed, and snorted at me expectantly, waking me from the half sleep I had settled into.

"Well, hi! What are you doing here, Des?"

She jumped up, rested her front paws on my mattress frame, and wagged her stump.

"Do you want to come up?" I laughed. Her legs were too short to propel her wrinkly body all the way. "Ok. I've got you." I sat up and moved to lift her. "Oof. You are considerably more solid than you look." I had to get out of bed and bend my knees for enough leverage to hoist her.

Once successfully boosted, Desmond snuggled immediately into the covers, which released a storm of short white fur into the air. When it landed on the comforter, I didn't mind. "You getting your winter coat, Des?" I lay back down as the dog released a long sigh and nuzzled her nose into my armpit, already asleep.

Desmond woke before I did, and when I opened my eyes, I found her nudging my buzzing phone with her nose and pressing her paw to my forearm. Terror gripped me as I looked at the screen and saw Rainbow's name, along with the time.

Why was she calling me at five in the morning? Images of gas leaks and overflowing dishwashers filled my head as I answered.

"Rainbow? What's wrong?"

"Climate change, war, alienation...but amidst it all, there is love."

"Rainbow. Why are you calling me at 5am?" My exasperated humph freed a clump of fur from the sheets, and I watched as it floated back to the bed.

"Is it five?" Rainbow laughed. "I've been up all night with my new deck. We connected instantly—the cards really feel like an extension of my body. I..."

"Rainbow!" I interrupted. "Why are you calling?"

She laughed again, amused at her own flightiness. "Because the cards spoke to me about you, darling. Clearly, in fact."

I rolled my eyes so hard, it was amazing I was able to lower them again. "I'll call you later." My finger hovered over the "end call" button.

"Wait."

I sighed. "What did it say?"

"There was a six of swords, of course." Rainbow had named me partially for this card, with its solemn passengers rowing toward a distant shore. She had always told me it represented taking control of one's own destiny and moving away from what didn't serve you, but when I had looked it up in seventh grade, the only explanations I could find were about unhappy transitions.

"The next card I pulled was Death. This deck imagines it as a laughing skull with a flower crown. It's really quite beautiful."

"Shit." Is that why the call was so urgent? I was far from a true believer in tarot, but regardless of my skepticism, the idea of someone foreseeing my end creeped me the hell out.

Rainbow laughed. "Not literal death." She paused. "Not necessarily."

"Thanks for the reassurance."

"It's about the death of a time in your life, or of a relationship, or an idea. Something big crumbles so something else can be reborn. It may be painful, but it is the beginning of something new."

"Does every tarot card actually mean the same thing? Isn't that essentially the six of swords ,too?"

"In a way, yes, but you know for me, the six of swords is always an indication the reading is for you, so I believe the Death card was driving home the meaning. Plus, as part of the Major Arcana, its message is more extreme—less a transition than a total transformation."

I had to admit the message felt relevant, but I also knew this was the reason people bought into this stuff. Any card could feel relevant at any given moment. I took in a deep breath and blew it out slowly.

"The final pull was quite different."

On the other end of the line, I could hear Rainbow tapping her fingers on the card like she always did. I could picture her perfectly, sitting in the dark before the coffee table in her caftan, the seventies coke bottle glasses she wore before putting in her contacts perched on the bridge of her nose. "The lovers. This deck is wonderfully inclusive—the people are of indeterminate gender."

"I'm glad you support my bisexuality, Rainbow, and no, I'm not hiding a secret girlfriend. What does the card mean?"

Beside me, Desmond yawned. It was contagious, and I stifled my own.

"Keep an open mind. And an open heart. Roger isn't trying to hurt you."

"I know."

"These cards together suggest there is new love in your life. You simply have to let it in. Move toward love."

My breath caught.

"And Sailor?"

Her words had struck a nerve, whether their pertinence was coincidental or not.

"Yeah?" My throat was tight, and I hoped she couldn't hear my sudden effort to hold back tears.

"Be crumbled. So wild flowers will come up where you are. You have been stony for too many years. Try something different. Surrender."

"Rumi?" I had to pinch my lips together to keep them from trembling.

"Of course."

"Thanks, Rainbow. Can I go back to sleep now?"

I focused on keeping my breathing deep and suppressing the whimper threatening to erupt at any moment.

"Rest well, little one."

I hung up and slid low under the blanket to shield my eyes from the sun beginning to come through the blinds.

Quietly, I let the tears come as I squeezed my fists, curled my body into a ball, and shook with silent sobs, like I didn't even want myself to know I had given in to crying. When I'd finally expelled my trembling heartache, I let my body lie still and felt my breath move in and out of my nostrils. Slowly, I uncurled and emerged from the covers.

"What do you think, Des?" I whispered. "It's bullshit, right?" The dog picked her head up and looked at me with indignation—like I had personally offended her.

"Oh, I'm sorry, pup!" I scratched her scruff until she rested her chin back onto the bed. "You think it means I should be open to love from you? Well, then, you're right. Definitely legit."

Hours later, the doorbell jolted me awake, but I stayed curled in bed, certain Roger would answer it. I vaguely registered that Desmond was no longer beside me, though she had left a flattened, furry bit of blanket in her place. I patted the space sleepily as I drifted back to sleep.

When the doorbell rang again, a series of short, rapping knocks followed it. I groaned, rolled to sitting, and reached up to feel the floppy bun on top of my head. My eyes felt puffy from crying, and my breath tasted like coffee though I hadn't had any since yesterday morning.

"Coming!" I shouted, though I took my time shuffling to the door. Maybe Roger had ordered something...more bags or packing paper. But as I threw open the door, expecting to find a delivery person, instead I found...

"Jake?"

Big bags hung under his eyes. He hadn't been sleeping well either. I fought the urge to reach for his face.

"Good thinking." He gestured my way. "You'll be cozy on the plane."

I looked down at my black jogger pants and sweatshirt, suddenly aware I had been wearing them for two days. Wait...the plane? He still wanted to go?

A muffled bark from the backyard snapped me out of my bewildered gape, and I turned to see Desmond and Roger outside. So that explained Roger's about-face regarding Jake. They must have talked.

Desmond watched me through the glass as she squatted in her usual poop spot while Roger studied the rose bushes, pretending he wasn't eavesdropping. I couldn't get on a plane right now. I wasn't packed. I wasn't showered. I wasn't on great terms with my travel partner. But here that travel partner was—acting like my going was a given. He had bought the tickets. And I *did* still want to find the album.

I had Desmond, I reminded myself. The trip could very well be an awkward mess, but either way, it would be over soon, and I would come back to a puppy who liked to snuggle and make creepy eye contact during bowel movements. And maybe if it wasn't a mess...I bit my lip. I couldn't let myself consider it yet. I'd gotten my hopes up too much lately.

Still, I couldn't help the way my stomach fluttered knowing Jake had come after me—seeing him standing right here in my doorway. It was all I had wanted after our first big fight. Back then, Jake had waited weeks before messaging to ask for forgiveness, and by then, my obstinance had settled in and refused to allow me to grant it.

But neither of us were stubborn kids anymore, and his presence here confirmed it. Maybe one stupid fight didn't mean things were over now. Maybe I could be mature too. I could at least try.

"You talked to Roger."

"Yeah." Jake smiled, but it was half-hearted.

"What's wrong?" My softening heart constricted again. Jake didn't want to take this trip either. He pitied me, or he felt some obligation. What if Roger had put him up to it? I wouldn't put it past my friend to threaten him. Roger had good intentions, but sometimes his protectiveness caused more problems than it solved. It was his generosity, after all, which had enabled me for so long. "You don't have to do this. We don't have to go." I was not going to let myself be someone's charity case, especially not Jake's. "I'll be fine. Don't worry about me."

His face fell. "No, it's not that. I know you'll be fine. You're...you."

I leaned against the doorway and put a hand on my hip. "Then what? Why should we go?"

As much as I wanted to assume good intentions, I was wary. Roger was right when he'd said Jake had broken me. Even if my best friend had let his guard down, I needed more reassurance.

Jake rubbed his lips together and considered his answer. "The tickets are nonrefundable." He looked past me at the floor, knowing his response was pathetic.

I laughed coldly. "Of course. No strings attached to your money as long as I don't waste it."

Jake cringed but didn't defend himself. I studied his face and found no animosity, no greed. He didn't pity me and he didn't actually care about the money either. Something else was going on, but I couldn't put my finger on it. My curiosity won out.

"Fine."

"Fine, you'll go?" Jake straightened.

What the hell. "I'll go."

Jake's eyes brightened, and I allowed myself a brief moment of direct contact before moving my gaze to the lower half of his face. This time his smile seemed less half hearted and more...swollen? Like really swollen, actually. Was he having some sort of allergic reaction?

"Are you ok? Like, your face?"

Jake's hand rose to his jaw. "It turns out I knocked a tooth loose at The Barn the other day. I had to have it splinted."

"Oh my God, I'm so sorry." I wasn't sure if I felt more guilty or relieved.

"It's fine." He smiled again, wider, but still pained, and looked at his watch. "But we have to go."

"Right! Um. Give me a minute." Leaving Jake in the doorway, I ran back to my room, threw some clothes into a bag along with my phone charger and toothbrush, and popped a piece of wintergreen gum into my mouth. Then I opened the sliding door to the backyard. Again, I asked myself if I was really doing this.

Desmond leapt to her feet, letting a final turd fall, and bounded over to me. Yes. I could do this. I would be cautious but open minded, and no matter what, I'd come back to this pup.

"I'm going to New York." I squatted to pet Desmond and looked up at Roger who was clapping his hands, barely able to contain his glee.

"Yeah, you are!"

"Also, I hate you. Why didn't you tell me?"

"I couldn't ruin the gesture." He grinned. "Have fuuuuun."

"Gesture?"

Roger clamped his lips shut and I rolled my eyes. "I hate you," I said again.

"Love you, have fun, see you soon!" Roger grinned.

"Love you too, asshole."

He squealed as I slid the door shut behind me.

"Ready?" Jake asked when I returned.

"Ready."

The dash to the airport was a blur, the only words between me and Jake logistical. We checked in, scrambled through security, speed-walked to our gate. We were the last ones on the plane, bumping clumsily down the aisle and apologizing to fellow passengers as we found our seats.

Finally, ten thousand feet in the air, I was able to take a breath.

SoCal looked even more beautiful from this height. Even the cookie cutter houses and smoggy freeways were like parts of an elaborate futuristic sculpture.

"Hey," Jake said. I turned and looked into his brown irises. "I'm really sorry. I was an asshole."

Was that what this was about? Was this an elaborate ploy to apologize? He needed me somewhere I couldn't run away so I'd hear him out?

But Jake's eyes were so pleading, so earnest, my anger was quickly fading. I hadn't been innocent in this either.

I shook my head. "I was an asshole too."

He took my hand and leaned his curly head on my shoulder. I tensed at the contact, the urge to lean my own head on him warring with the instinct to squirm away.

But Jake was asleep within seconds. With the white noise of the plane and the warmth of Jake's breath on my collarbone, my own eyes soon drifted closed too. We could talk later—I'd suss out his intentions after I got a little rest. For now, this was fine.

I woke up to the snack cart rumbling by. "Peanuts?" asked the flight attendant.

"Yes, please." I took two bags from the man and handed one to Jake, who was already awake and nervously twiddling his thumbs.

"I don't think I can eat those with my mouth hardware." He brought a hand to his cheek, which seemed to have swelled even more.

"Aren't you hungry?" I asked.

"Very. Approaching hangry."

"I'm sorry." Internally, I growled at my automatic sympathy. I still wasn't sure if he deserved it.

"No worries. I should have packed snacks or something. Something soft."

"We'll get you something as soon as we land," I promised.

As if on command, our plane began to descend gently through the clouds, which parted in its wake, and New York City appeared below, like a densely packed game board. When I wiggled my jaw to adjust the pressure in my ears, I realized my mouth had been hanging wide open.

Jake echoed my thoughts. "Wow."

I had never seen anything like it. There was the Statue of Liberty. There was the Brooklyn Bridge. Recognizable landmarks, suddenly real, and yet so small from this vantage point I felt like I could pluck them up with two fingers. It was the most beautiful thing I had ever seen. I suddenly regretted only having a day here when there was so much to see.

I had almost missed this.

But the beauty pulled something in my chest, made it unravel like a loose sweater string. It was a beauty that could never be mine—a beauty luring Roger away from me.

I kept my eyes glued to the window. "It's kind of ugly."

"Are we seeing the same thing?" Jake asked as we descended further. "Did you see the Bridge?" He pointed, and I worked hard to look unimpressed.

We continued staring as the plane moved lower and lower, my heart thumping hard as we approached. It was a steeper decline than most flights I'd been on, as I guessed it had to be, given the tall buildings, and being an island and all. Excitement and tension competed within me as the runway drew near, and when the wheels finally touched down, I exhaled, fighting the urge to shove my way to the front of the plane to make the most of the few hours we had in the city.

"We'll have to come back sometime," Jake said, like he sensed my anxiety. But his words revealed the real source of my tension—it wasn't only New York I was worried about soaking up—it was Jake. I knew this trip would make or break us, and I was desperate to make the most of whatever time we had.

"Let's get some food in you. Low blood sugar is probably not ideal for figuring out public transit."

Fifteen minutes later, we were in the airport holding bagels. "Oh my God," I said, as my mouth met the combination of fresh doughy bread and roughly a pound of cream cheese.

"Oh my God," Jake agreed.

He was only chewing on one side of his mouth.

"Does it hurt?"

"It's soft enough to manage," he said through a bite. "And the taste more than makes up for it. I always kind of thought people were bullshitting when they hyped up New York bagels, but I stand corrected."

Around us, people hurried by without sparing a single glance in our direction. A woman with an expensive-looking handbag talked loudly into her cell phone, her accent so strong, she seemed like a caricature. A man walked hand in hand with a kid in a full superhero costume. A group of seniors in matching "Big Apple Forever" shirts forced the crowd to part. In the space of a minute, I heard people speaking Spanish, Chinese, and German.

Jake and I were completely anonymous here, and yet instantly integrated into the hustle, even as tourists. It would have been overwhelming on my own, but with Jake here, I was ready to explore—to squeeze every drop I could from this experience.

I had never felt so at home somewhere in my life, and we hadn't even left La Guardia.

Guard, I thought, the airport's name reminding me. The hope I felt here, the excitement, meant it was even more important to guard my heart.

CHAPTER 19: JAKE

It was truly remarkable what good food did for my mood.

Sailor's walls had been up since I'd appeared in her doorway, and I couldn't blame her. Even after we'd apologized on the plane, I could feel her holding back, and her comments about New York being ugly had made me wonder if this was a terrible idea—if by dragging us across the country, I was prolonging the inevitable. Maybe no gesture, however grand, could make up for me being a hurtful dick.

But the bagel had shifted something in both of us, even though my jaw was exhausted from only chewing on one side. I could think more clearly when my stomach wasn't attempting to eat itself, but that wasn't the whole story. It was cheesy, but the taste and texture—so new and delicious, had felt like a metaphor. Sailor and I still had so much to discover together.

Had I discovered a single thing in the years we'd been apart?

I saw the change in her, too, while she ate—her face started to remind me of her seventeen-year-old self—the one who showed up when we were alone or with our bandmates—silly, excited, open to the world.

Bit by bit, she opened up. She lightened up. I was still chewing my last bite when Sailor took my hand and dragged me to a transit map. The schema was gibberish—a tangle of colored lines, letters, numbers, and names I'd never heard of.

"So the old CBGB is here." Sailor pointed to the section of the map labeled "Manhattan." "And I think Arlene's Grocery is, too. We should do those before we go to Queens for Danger."

"You take a cartography class at Chaffey?" *Dammit, Jake. Maybe don't bring up our sore spots when things are starting to look up.* "You're a regular Ernest Shackleton." I raised my voice and pointed at Sailor. "Amelia Earhart over here, people!"

Sailor smiled as she swatted at my outstretched finger. Then she shrugged. "Your brain remembered musicians' names, mine remembered essential music history locations."

"I'm impressed."

But as she went back to studying the map, Sailor's face fell. "I wish we had time for a show. I'd love to see something at The Bowery Ballroom. And online, people say Bar Freda is a great new space."

It took everything in me not to tell her the show back home would be worth the quick trip. "How do we get to Manhattan?" I asked instead.

The Link Q70-SBS bus's various shades of blue were like a 90s ad, its cram of passengers reminiscent of a mosh pit. I had no idea how Sailor made out the mumbled words of the driver as he announced each stop over his mic, but I trusted her as she dragged me back down the aisle and out to the Roosevelt and 74th Street Station.

The cold didn't have time to permeate my hoodie before we descended into the underground station. It was like a sci-fi movie—all steel and glass. Sailor traversed it confidently, and I followed like an obedient puppy.

"Let me get it," I said, as we stood before the ticketing machine calculating how many single rides we'd have to take to make the seven-day pass worth it. Behind us, a dude in a suit tapped his foot.

"Sorry, man." I gave him an apologetic smile.

"You literally paid for everything else. I'll spend the, like, twenty bucks. Besides." Sailor twitched her head in the direction of the impatient businessman. "My card is already out."

If I'd thought buying passes was our biggest challenge, actually getting to the train proved me wrong. Sailor and I clambered up and down stairs several times trying to find the right subway, headed in the right direction.

"I always wanted to be a contestant on *Legends of the Hidden Temple* when I watched those reruns as a kid," I panted, when we finally arrived at the correct platform—which of course was the one where we had started.

Sailor moved toward the track, toes right against the yellow line, and stared down into the grimy pit. "How do people not constantly die on these tracks?"

I joined her and lined my toes up by hers, wondering if the move reminded Sailor of marching band, too. "You're thinking of *Nickelodeon Guts*. I think the Aggro Crag was steeper, but the higher stakes here might give it a similar feel."

Sailor laughed. "I wasn't talking about a game show. Isn't it weird there are so many people here and such an obvious way to murder someone, but it still rarely happens? It makes me reconsider my stance on humans."

"That question makes me reconsider my stance on a particular human. Should I be worried?"

Sailor let out a belly laugh, then narrowed her eyes in an exaggerated sinister sneer.

I mimed concern, but inside I was beaming.

Outwardly, Sailor had always been a cynic, but I had seen this side of her shine through before, in moments when she was at her happiest—the first time we listened to a new song or the day on the roof of the gas station.

I loved Sailor the skeptic, but I hated the pain closing herself off to the world had brought her, and I'd felt guilty since my chat with Roger, convinced I had confirmed her tendency toward negativity forever. But now, right next to me, was that glimmer of openheartedness again. I would do anything to preserve it.

The train pulled into the station with a gust loud enough to shut up my inner monologue, and my heart leapt into my throat. Sailor grabbed my hand and pulled me through the sliding doors. Inside, the car was packed. Two Orthodox men sat side by side on the twin orange seats looking like twins themselves. Beside them, a man in a yarmulke held the hand of a little girl with blonde ringlets and a backpack as she used her other hand to shovel crackers into her mouth. A pair of teenagers made out passionately by the door on the other side, the boy with one hand grasping the metal pole and the other hand grabbing his girlfriend's ass.

Beside me, Sailor, who hadn't let go of my hand, stared up at the scrolling marquee announcing each stop. In here, from my plastic seat, the subway propelling us toward Manhattan, the chaos was less overwhelming. As I held Sailor's hand and took it all in, it was actually strangely comforting. I squeezed Sailor's hand gently, and she turned to meet my eyes.

"I like being in New York with you," I said.

"I like being in New York with you, too."

A muffled voice came over the speaker.

"That's us."

"If you say so." I let Sailor guide me through the crowd.

CBGB was really nothing to look at, but still, as we stood in front of the awning—no longer its iconic white with red letters, but black and neat, the name of a designer printed across it, it was like I could feel the ghosts of all the music legends who had been here before.

Choking Victim, The Toasters, Patti Smith. They'd all stood right here. I tried to breathe it in, but before the air could reach the bottom of my lungs, a lady with a giant leather bag bumped into me, sending me flying to the edge of the sidewalk. For a moment, my breath caught, as a stream of people flowing between us blocked Sailor from view, but as the crowd parted, I saw her searching face light up as she found me.

The five feet between us felt like an ocean, and I crossed it determinately, putting my head down to wind between the fast-walking crowd and get to the beautiful woman on the other side.

I grabbed Sailor's hand. "Phew. I felt like a kid lost at the mall there for a second."

"I felt like a parent who lost her kid at the mall."

"I'm glad we both recognize how incompetent I am." I laughed. The role reversal was good for us, though. I knew Sailor was self-conscious about our different lives, and it was nice to be in a setting where she was the confident one. I would let her lead, I decided, for this whole trip.

Sailor gave an exaggerated cringe, then grew serious. "As long as I don't lose you again."

Tears misted my vision. "I don't want to lose you again either."

"Then let's not lose each other again."

As we leaned in to kiss, the world telescoped, closing in until it was just us and the famous awning in focus. We were part of this place's history forever now, like it was part of ours. It was irreversible, and the thought made me want to do something impulsive, something drastic— jump naked into the Central Park fountain or get matching tattoos.

The rush of traffic and humans were a blurred backdrop. Every one of these people had their own complex inner lives and interpersonal dramas, but in this moment, Sailor and I were the main characters.

Finally, Sailor drew back from our embrace. "What famous people do you think have made out in this exact spot?"

"Hm. Hulk Hogan, Betty White—"

Sailor guffawed. "You goof."

"Oh!" I feigned. "I didn't mean Hulk and Betty with each other. My bad. Individually. With other people."

Sailor smirked and shook her head in faux disapproval. "You're ridiculous." She kissed me again.

In my mind's eye, I had a bird's eye view of the island, like a subway map without the lines, Sailor and I pulsing where we stood like a neon thumbtack. As we stood under the awning, full-on frenching, not a single person told us to "get a room" or even cat called. We were perfectly integrated into the landscape—another thing happening in a city of sensory overload—the only defense, to block most of it out.

Speaking of blocking out... "What is that smell?" I pulled away.

"What—" Sailor started, before the scent hit her too. "Oh, God." She clasped both hands over her nose. "It's like something died."

I spotted the rat right as she said it.

"Something did die." I pointed to the rodent, its little legs and tail peeking out from under a giant trash bag like the Wicked Witch of the East. "I always thought the rat thing was a stereotype."

We stared as a pigeon swooped down and began pecking at a hole in the bag directly over where the rat lay, then stepped on the creature in order to get a better view.

"Time to go?" Sailor asked. I nodded as she laced her fingers through mine. I'd go anywhere this woman took me.

★ ★ ★ ★ ★ ★ ★

APRIL 15, 2013

xDrummerChickx: Jake told me he wants to go to Berkeley

GaYrUdEbOySUnItE: I know. His mom hasn't stopped talking about how she hopes he gets in

xDrummerChickx: ugh. is it just her pressuring him then?

GaYrUdEbOySUnItE: idk :/

xDrummerChickx: we're gonna make this show epic. he'll see he cares more about the band than whatever his mom wants him to do

CHAPTER 20: SAILOR

I'd learned about Arlene's Grocery from The Fenwicks, who had released their live album from the bodega-turned-club in 2002. It was within walking distance, and I was glad for the chance to stretch my legs, though as we hurried through narrow streets, the tall buildings acted as a tunnel for the icy wind, and I longed for the enclosure of the subway system. "I have never been this cold in my life." I held tight to Jake's hand for warmth as well as security.

"How is it this fucking cold?" Jake chattered. Neither of us were dressed for the weather. All around us, New Yorkers wore puffy black knee-length coats, scarves, gloves, and even earmuffs, while Jake and I shivered in our paltry California winter gear. At least I had a beanie, thin as it was. I was worried Jake's curls might freeze and break off.

As we passed cafes and barber shops, bars and restaurants, it was hard to process the sheer number of things in one place, not to mention people. If our trip was longer, and if it hadn't been under twenty degrees, I would have wanted to take my time and stop in each place to feel its vibe and watch the people who went to each one. How did people pick a favorite spot in a place with so many options? The excess of cultural riches felt unfathomable.

"Oh shit, Rockwood Music Hall." Jake pointed to a sign coming up on our left. "And a vegan restaurant next-door."

I'd heard about Rockwood too, and hadn't even realized it was on our route. For a moment, I wondered what my life would be like if I lived here—if I had always lived here.

It wasn't unreasonable—my great grandparents had come to Ellis Island from Czecho-slovakia. If my Bubbie Lindy hadn't decided to move to California to try to be a movie star, I probably would have lived here. Though if my Bubbie Lindy hadn't moved to California, she wouldn't have met Zadie Howard and had my mom. And then my mom wouldn't have met my dad at a Zen retreat in Joshua Tree, they wouldn't have banged under the stars, and then I probably wouldn't *be* at all.

I sighed at the thought of my mom. Even leaving her for a couple days had made me nervous, but at least Roger was still nearby in case of emergency. I forced myself to feel the cold—to really absorb it—as we walked past Rockwood. It was cold in New York. Who would want to live in the cold?

Finally, we arrived in front of Arlene's, and in spite of our entwined fingers, my hand was almost numb. I dislodged from Jake and shoved it into my pocket, desperate for a bit more warmth.

A sign proclaiming "Fresh music, cold beer" adorned the brightly painted red and yellow building. A ramp led to a boxy entryway, which looked like a cross between a London phone box and Charlie's glass elevator. The atmosphere reminded me of the California ghost town we had visited on a seventh grade field trip—abandoned, but haunted and creepily preserved. It was somehow an eerier feeling in the middle of Manhattan than it was in the desert.

My phone buzzed and I glanced quickly at the screen. Rainbow. Of course. If I hadn't been the skeptic of the family, I would think I'd summoned her with my thoughts.

Then my throat thickened. The dryer. She'd forgotten to clean the lint trap again, and this time it had caught fire. What if her house was gone? What if it wasn't her at all, but a neighbor or a firefighter trying to reach me because...

Chill, Sailor.

I opened the message and read—"Toilet won't stop running. Jiggled handle repeatedly, still wasting precious water."

I exhaled in relief, then groaned, preparing to call a plumber and schedule an appointment from 3000 miles away.

"Everything alright?" Jake asked, and the concern in his voice shifted something in me. Everything was alright. This was not an emergency. My mother was an adult, and she could figure this out on her own. I swiped the text away and put my phone back without responding.

"All good." I returned my stare to the dark building before us.

"Is it open?" Jake was trying to peek around show posters to peer into a dark window. I examined the flyers. They were recent—all for upcoming shows, though they peeled in the corner like they'd been slapped up hastily.

I thought guiltily of the photo of Pauline Black I had ripped from my wall.

There was a show tonight, I saw—hardcore punk from the looks of it, but I didn't care. My extremities warmed at the idea of seeing a show here, standing so close to the band, letting the giant amps on the stage immerse me in the experience, and my heart sank as I remembered how quick our mission was.

"I'm about to invoke squatters' rights if it isn't." I climbed the ramp and pushed gently at the door. To my relief, it opened.

Inside was dark, save for floodlights pointed toward a stage. Tables and barstools lined both sides. There were no signs of life. I was reconsidering our intrusion when the curtains behind the stage rustled and a petite woman emerged wearing painter's coveralls and platform combat boots.

"Show's not til eight. Or are you with one of the bands?" Her nasal accent was so extreme, I thought she might be faking it.

"No. We're just visiting," Jake said.

I jumped in. "We are musicians." I wanted this woman to know I belonged—that we had a common language. "But we're not playing here."

"Well, do ya wanna beer or ya just gawking?" She was unimpressed, probably annoyed we had disrupted whatever she was doing in the back.

"Sure," I said. It suddenly felt important to have an authentic experience in New York aside from the bagels. The woman stepped off the stage and went to a small refrigerator where she retrieved two bottles of Red Stripe—something else I only knew of through ska—and handed them to us. We stood by the wooden bar along the wall and popped the tops.

When I took a drink, it tasted like any other lager, but I reminded myself it hailed from Jamaica, and was loved by so many ska bands, several had even named themselves after it.

Jake took a sip and squinted as he nodded in appreciation. "Mm."

"Twenty dollars." The woman held out her hand.

I choked as Jake handed the woman his card. Another thing to dislike about New York. California was expensive, but not usually $10 beer expensive.

I pushed down my guilt at my increasing tab. Jake had sworn I didn't owe him. I took another slug as the venue's steward disappeared backstage again.

"I'm already tipsy," Jake said.

My brows raised. We'd never been drinkers in high school—alcohol was too enmeshed in the popular kids' scene—but I'd assumed Jake had occasionally indulged as an adult. Especially in college. "Lightweight."

"All I've had is a bagel!" he protested. "And nothing before the bagel since lunch yesterday. I was too sore."

At least it wasn't Hillary's influence that had led him to temperance.

"Aww." I smoothed my thumb gently over his swollen jaw, but pulled back when he winced.

"It's fine." He reached out to stroke my cheek, mirroring my gesture. His hand was still cold from outside, but I couldn't help tilting into his caress. "It's worth it. I'd take more pain—like ten times the pain, to end up right here with you."

Words had always come so easy for Jake. I wanted to tell him I felt the same way—that even the waiting had been worth it, and maybe we had needed that time to understand how much we meant to each other. You would think, with a mom like mine, sharing emotions would be easy. But the words wouldn't come.

Part of me was still too scared—too sure something would go wrong.

Jake went on. "Sailor, I hope you know how serious I am about this. I've known since our first day on the band bus I loved you."

I looked down. "You *are* tipsy."

"Yes." Jake smiled, then grew serious again. "But I mean it. I want to make a life with you, whatever you want that life to look like. Hell, you can knock into me with a door once a week if you want. I'd prefer not."

I couldn't help but giggle at the playful glint in his eyes as they reflected the floodlights.

"We can do monthly," I said.

"Deal."

We were quiet for a minute before I spoke again. "Me too." Maybe my own lack of food was affecting my alcohol tolerance, but something in me was opening. "I want a life with you, too."

Before Jake could respond, the woman appeared again, warmer than before, maybe because she had registered Jake's large tip. She approached, and her stance widened as she leaned an elbow on the bar, looking us over from head to toe.

"Irene," she said. Apparently whatever she had been doing backstage hadn't been too pressing.

As we sipped from our stubby bottles, Irene filled us in on the state of New York City music venues as I tried and failed to peel the screen printed label off my bottle. Everywhere was struggling, Irene said, even places like Arlene's, which had been around forever.

"Since 1995. But we'll be gone by February if something doesn't change. We've got folks sending money and shit, but that won't cut it. Without regular crowds like we used to have, it's only a matter of time."

I thought of CBGBs and its revamped facade—all the character and history painted over like it was nothing. A bubble of inspiration reached my blood at the same time as the alcohol. I could help Arlene's get back on its feet—book bands, get people excited about live music again.

But no. I already had a mission. This one was Irene's.

"What are you going to do?" I asked.

Irene's smile was sad but she lifted her chin. "Keep playing music. As long as we can."

I recognized myself in this woman. I straightened my spine, our shared commitment fortifying my resolve.

I felt Jake's arm wrap around my waist, and his touch further steeled me. Maybe he got it now.

So what if it had taken a stranger to show him my devotion to music wasn't silly? Right now I didn't care. We were on the same team again. And we had a mission.

Downing the last of my Red Stripe, I slammed it with a bit too much force onto the counter. "Sorry. We have to get to Queens."

But Irene had already swept the bottle into a plastic tub. She took another look at our clothes. "Good luck out there," she said.

I pulled my beanie down over my ears as I headed toward the door. "You, too," I called over my shoulder.

The cold hit like a wall as we opened the door. "Is that snow?" Jake squinted into the sky.

"Fuck." I caught a flake on the arm of my hoodie. We linked arms and, heads down, walked out into the Lower East Side. The wind howled as fiercely as it had on the walk from CBGB's, but somehow I didn't feel as cold. I had wanted a real experience, and I had gotten one. Even better, Jake had been there too.

I was ready for more.

CHAPTER 21: JAKE

I didn't mind the chill—not with Sailor next to me. Hell, with the right clothes, I might even be able to enjoy it. I was used to being aware of my body when I was self-conscious about it, but with the cold, I could feel my physical presence in the world without judging it. I could sense the outline of myself, but the awareness combined with the anonymity of the city. No one else was judging me. The dissociation I felt at work, when I drove, when I sat around a dinner table with people I didn't like—this was the opposite.

I only wished we could stay here longer—me and Sailor, alone in this giant city, far from noisy freeways and nosy families. If only there was a way to make money out here.

Then I remembered. "Jerome Higgins." It could really work.

"I'm Sailor." She smirked. "And you really are a lightweight."

She wasn't wrong. The single beer had made me comfortable and happy. Everything seemed to have a slight shine. I probably did need lunch. I wondered if we had time to stop for pizza.

"I know you're Sailor." I had to jog to match her pace. "I could never forget who you are."

I stopped suddenly, and our linked hands forced Sailor to pause, too. People rushed around as I leaned over and puckered my lips, and though she laughed at me again, she leaned in for a kiss. It was like one of those time lapse videos where the main subjects move in real time while everything around them goes at 10x.

"Move, breeders!" a man shouted as he pushed past.

I turned to see the person we had annoyed was wearing a purple cowboy hat atop his otherwise conservative business attire. On the street, taxis and busses zipped past, honking and weaving.

Another man glared as he lifted a small dog over his head to get by, exaggerating how little space he had to move around us, as he muttered, "Jesus Christ."

I guided us to a shop entrance, where we huddled close to the wall. You couldn't stand still in this part of New York.

"What about Jerome Higgins?" Sailor asked.

A man with a blue mohawk walked past, followed by a woman in a full ball gown. No one batted an eye at either of them. I looked into the window of the business we stood before and saw it was a sex shop. Mannequins in red feather boas and leather chaps stood beside displays of enormous dildos, some of which were shaped like tails or tentacles. God, I loved New York.

"Uh...cool," I said, momentarily distracted by the colorful sex toys. "Anyway...Jerome Higgins! I forgot! He's hiring a legal guy for his nonprofit. It's a weird fuckin' coincidence, right? What if we moved out here? We'd be close to Roger and all this music and..." I gestured toward the window with a smirk, expecting a laugh from Sailor. Instead, she stared at me, her brow creasing. "I'm sure it's easier to find drum students here, too. And all the venues, even if they are struggling. You could help them get back on their feet! Ska forever!" I leaned in for another kiss, but Sailor took a step back and bumped into a small Asian woman emerging from the store.

"Sorry," Sailor blurted, then turned back to me. "Really Jake? Still?"

"Still what?"

Was she worried I'd delayed our trip to the subway? Was she upset I was keeping us out in the cold?

"You're still trying to get me to leave. To convince me you would be better at designing my life."

Suddenly, I was one hundred percent sober. "Designing your life? I thought you liked it here."

"What gave you that idea? Was it when I said it was ugly? Or when I said I hated the cold?"

"I may not have excelled at Berkeley but I did ok in Psych 101. I know you, Sailor. Those were defense tactics."

"So what if they were? You assumed I wanted to move here? Quite a leap." She crossed her arms and I mirrored the gesture.

All at once, the cold was painful. All at once, I was the fat guy in everyone's way. All at once, I was back in high school and Sailor was losing her shit again. "I didn't think you'd freak about me imagining it, at least. Why are you pissed at me? I'm trying to help you. I'm trying to imagine a situation where you can incorporate music into real life."

"Imagine away, Jake. You clearly have never understood me."

Never understood her? Sailor was the person I'd thought I understood best in this world.

"What are you talking about? I heard you—you want to play professionally, no compromises. I support you. I'm in, fully."

"You thought that's all it was about? My staying in SoCal?" Sailor was looking at me like I was a stranger, her eyes darting back and forth.

"Wasn't it? The rest of the band was there and…"

"They weren't there. You and Hillary left. I'd figured we'd have to replace her, but you…We missed out on touring because of you. Do you think anyone felt like practicing after? What was the point?"

I closed my mouth, which had been hanging open.

I'd known the band had dissolved, but I didn't know it had been so immediate. If Sailor hadn't stuck around to try to make the band work, then why…

"We fell apart after. Sonia, Romero, and Go all went their own way. All the momentum disappeared. Roger and I tried finding other people to play with for awhile, but it was no use. No one else had the chemistry we did, and my heart wasn't in it anymore."

"Then why did you stay? We could have made up…you could have come to Berkeley…I waited for you for a year." My voice cracked with the admission, and the realization Sailor and I may have had a second chance long ago. This was our *second* second shot…and we were ruining it, too.

"I didn't only want to stay for the band." Sailor's arms fell to her sides. "I wanted the band to succeed so badly because I thought it would make you stay. I have to be in SoCal. I can't leave my mom. I don't know how you couldn't see that. It's like you never really saw me."

The look on her face killed me, but I didn't only feel guilty now. I was pissed. What did Rainbow have to do with her staying? How was I supposed to know things she'd never told me?

"I'm not a mindreader, Sailor." I threw my own hands into the air. "How was I supposed to know the reason? You didn't mention Rainbow once when we fought at The Barn, or ever, really. Whenever I mentioned her, you changed the subject."

Suddenly a flashback struck—the first time I'd met Alan and Belinda Deckland—how Hillary had prepped me, picking out what I should wear, telling me what topics to avoid. How, once there, she had gone out of her way to talk for and over me—glossing over my Judaism, my mediocre GPA.

Now, I saw Sailor had felt the same way. She'd been embarrassed to introduce me to her mom, hadn't she?

"And you never invited me to your house—you thought your mom would be disappointed in your vanilla boyfriend."

"You didn't have to read my mind!" Sailor was yelling again, and in my peripheral vision, people passing by were giving us covert looks, trying to hear what we were arguing about. "You just had to pay attention to me—not your idea of me as your manic pixie ska girl, but me—what I was actually dealing with."

She huffed and turned her eyes skyward. "And I wasn't embarrassed of you...I was embarrassed of her. Your house was so clean, and your mom acted like an actual adult. I didn't want you to see what a weirdo Rainbow really was."

Pay attention to her? All I had ever done was pay attention to Sailor.

I had observed her like a scientist—analyzed everything she said, every move she made. Our whole relationship had essentially been me worshipping her. Sure, she asked questions about me, too, but now I thought about it, she had always mocked my answers. I had thought it was lighthearted, teasing, but right now, it felt sinister.

"Because you clearly cared what was happening between me and my mom," I spat. "All you saw was some perfect mother archetype. Why do you think *I* wanted to leave so badly? Why do you think I'm dreaming of New York now? You thought I was afraid of her judgment. You never thought maybe I needed a way out?"

The irony hit me. We'd both lacked the courage to stand up to our moms.

Sailor's expression changed from angry to genuinely thoughtful for a moment, before swinging back to pissed. "Fine, Jake. Apply to work for Higgins. Move to New York. I won't hold you back."

"You're not..." I stopped. How could I correct her? She wasn't holding me back. I didn't want to work for Higgins just to work for him. I'd proposed it for both of us—a way to be here together, to be closer to venues like Arlene's.

But that wouldn't explain why I had missed the reason she'd wanted to stay in the first place—how I had assumed she wanted to escape her mother the same way I did—how I'd missed her being a better person than me.

But Sailor had looked past me, too. She had used our band to try to manipulate me into staying—into missing out on a good school and staying stuck at home.

I knew for certain what I had tried to deny ten years earlier when I'd admitted to Hillary how Sailor mocked me for listening to popular bands sometimes. I had glossed over it in my missing her, and pushed it down these last few days when her jokes jostled my insecurities.

Maybe I had idolized Sailor, but now I could see it clearly—she had tried to mold me into the cool boyfriend she'd wanted, the same way Hillary had tried to lead me in the other direction.

I let out a frustrated sigh. Roger was going to kill me. Right now, though, it was the least of my worries. Right now, I was on an island with a person who hated me, with a pointless mission and a plane to catch.

"What do we do now?" I asked as I shrugged my shoulders. Part of me wanted to call it. We could go home, cancel the show. I'd tell the band there was no reunion song.

But that wasn't fair. Sonia had been genuinely excited, and she'd said Romero and Go would be, too. I wanted to be less isolated. I really had missed my friends. And we were already here. I'd already blown half my savings on this absurd scheme.

Sailor shrugged back.

"I guess we better go get Jimmy Danger," I said.

"You mean the sad old musician?"

"Him," I confirmed.

"We're running late." Sailor's face was expressionless. Silently, she began to speed walk in the direction of the subway as I followed, still jogging to keep up.

From: Jesse Diaz-Ortega

Sent: April 19, 2013 10:15 AM

To: Jimmy Danger, Jerry Danger, Tony Danger, Sammy Danger, Petey Danger, Jamie Danger

Subject: Summer/Fall Opener

Hey guys,

Just checking in. I'm working on booking venues, but some places want me to list all the touring bands. You guys locked down an opener? You said you were thinking about those kids in SoCal. Let me know ASAP.

Jesse

***

From: Jerry Danger

Sent: April 19, 2013 2:45 PM

To: Jesse Diaz-Ortega , Jimmy Danger, Tony Danger, Sammy Danger, Petey Danger, Jamie Danger

Subject: Re: Summer/Fall Opener

Hey Jess—

The Skankin' Kiddos didn't work out. They kicked ass but we may have caused some drama. Jimmy invited them on the tour and their trombone player said he couldn't do it because he'd be at college. The drummer totally flipped. Broke her drums and everything. Fucking nuts. We'll find someone though.

Jerry

CHAPTER 22: SAILOR

The subway smelled like feet. Or maybe mustard. Mustard on feet. Why were people's feet so sweaty in this weather?

I almost said as much to Jake before remembering I wasn't speaking to him. It was the kind of comment he would appreciate, and the inability to share it with him brought a fresh stab of pain to my chest.

And still, even with the aroma of condiments and sweaty extremities, even with the ache of knowing Jake and I had tried and failed, again, to make it work, I couldn't help my exhilaration. Every minute in New York was new—a constant swirling menagerie of people combining, separating, and recombining in different configurations to create new situations.

I loved how unpredictable it was. How I felt simultaneously like an observer and like one of the variables affecting each moment. How I was totally separate from my daily life and my history and obligations. How no one knew me, but the possibility lurked everywhere that they could. That I could be someone here.

But I couldn't. Not really. Rainbow needed me, and as skeptical as I tried to be about all of her superstitions, I couldn't help but feel by talking about it out loud, I had created some emergency. I checked my phone anxiously before remembering the lack of service underground.

The train screeched to its next stop and the momentum made my arm brush against Jake's, which caused me to tear up almost instantly. I could never be what he wanted, and he would never truly understand why. Part of me wanted to explain—to remind him of the little things he'd found so amusing when we were kids—the crystals found in my backpack, the way I printed all of my homework in purple ink because Rainbow repeatedly forgot to replace our cartridge—and help him put the pieces together. The other part of me was still furious he hadn't seen it.

Of course I couldn't expect him to read my mind. I knew that wasn't fair. But I had thought he could read *me*. I'd thought he knew me well enough to sense something was off, could decipher the reticence in my laugh when other members of our band commented on how cool it was my mom smoked pot or how they wished their parents didn't believe in the concept of curfews.

Hadn't he wondered why I was fine with always hanging out at his house? Why I never invited my mom to marching band award dinners? Why, even now, when he had seemingly made peace with his own mom, I still tensed up whenever mine came up? I didn't expect him to read my mind, no, but I had expected him to pay attention.

I was so lost in thought, I almost missed our stop, and we had to rush to beat the closing doors. The momentum of the crowd pushed us out of the station and into the cold air. This part of New York was different than what we'd seen so far. The buildings were smaller, and some of the residences were actual houses. We passed a deli and grocery and a place whose awning advertised "Reggae Music, Costume Jewelry, Accessories."

"Damn, I wish we had more time to check that place out," Jake said, echoing my thoughts, and again, I regretted the tension between us.

Walking around Jamaica, Queens, it was clear we should have spent the whole day here. Further down the block, a man sat on a bench playing trumpet. Colorful murals adorned many of the buildings' walls. A man walked down the sidewalk, which was significantly less crowded than those on the East Side, in Rasta gear, his dreads far past his waist.

Maybe if we'd gone here first the fight never would have happened. Maybe we would have spent the day trawling through records and laughing. But then I wouldn't have known how Jake really saw me. It was probably better to know.

"I guess you can see how someone would start playing ska, living here." I looked back at the map on my phone. "Speaking of which, we're almost there. It's a left at the next block."

Jimmy Danger's house was old and narrow, with faded white paint and a half-fallen wire fence. Its small stoop was littered with beer bottles—mostly Red Stripe with a few Bud Lights thrown in for good measure. The door's paint was faded too, but looked to have once been a bright red.

Jake stood in front of the house like he was waiting to be let in, but when I stepped over the gate and began to climb the brick steps to the stoop, he followed, glancing in each direction.

"Will neighbors be weirded out by strangers going up to the house like this?"

I shrugged. Jake's cowardice—his unwillingness to take risks, was particularly annoying at the moment. Thankfully, no one seemed to notice our intrusion, and I was able to congratulate myself for my brazenness.

"No doorbell." I reached for the knob, but before I could touch it, Jake reached his hand over my shoulder and rapped hard three times on the now-orange door.

Finally, some initiative. If we'd been on good terms, I would have teased him about it, maybe given him a pat on the back. Instead, we waited, with the sound of the trumpet still faint in the distance, but there was no answer.

I knocked again. "Jimmy!" I called, with my hands cupped around my mouth, but after what felt like forever, there was still no response. Jake looked nervously at his fitness watch. I would have teased him about that too, if I was in a good mood. Instead, I noted it read over 12,000 steps. With that, plus the lack of sleep and the travel, no wonder I was exhausted. I also saw we had an hour and a half to get to the airport—not a lot of time to mess around.

Jake broke the silence. "I am not about to waste my whole savings, drag you across the country, and blow it again for nothing." He took a deep breath before ramming his shoulder hard into the wooden door. The words were as much of a bombshell as his sudden action.

"Ow," Jake cried. The door didn't budge.

Sheepishly, I reached again for the knob. It turned, and I suppressed my smirk. Not being able to rag on Jake was the hardest part of being so angry with him. I missed our playful dynamic.

The inside of Jimmy Danger's house smelled like beer and cat food. Show flyers hung haphazardly on the walls—glossy posters full of checkerboards and fedoras.

"Jimmy?" I called out. Someone stirred upstairs. "Jimmy?" I tried again.

"Who's there?" The voice came from upstairs.

I ascended the narrow steps with Jake following behind. The top opened to a small landing with an open bathroom door on the right and what I presumed was a bedroom on the left. I knocked.

"What? Fucking hell, what?" It was definitely Jimmy Danger in there. I pushed the door and let it swing open.

Beside me, Jake let out a low whistle.

I'd thought I'd given up my illusions about my former idol, but as my eyes took in the ska vocalist's disgusting bedroom, whatever remained fell away, lost somewhere on the floor amidst dirty glasses, cat hair, and scattered porn DVDs.

Jake picked up the one closest to my feet. "*Camel Toe Hoes 4*. Any good? Or did they jump the shark at 3?"

I couldn't stop the cackle that burst from my lips.

Jimmy Danger looked up from where he sat hunched over on the bed, his eyes brightening when they met mine. "You're that kid. You're the kid who flipped out." His now-wrinkled face looked ridiculous with his bleach blond hair, and he was so scrawny his button-up shirt hung off of him. It was hard to believe I'd looked up to him so much—cared so much what he'd thought of me leading up to, and following, our show at The Barn.

I steeled myself, determined not to recoil. "Yup, and you've clearly done well with your life. Come on." The truth behind my insult probably stung me more than it did him. He really was sad, and he really was clinging to his glory days. It actually was pathetic, and I could easily slip into this life myself.

I thought about the photo still lying on my floor at home. Wasn't that how it started—you let one thing slide and then more and more, until one day you're living in your head, the space around you covered in filth? This was what Roger worried about for me. This is what Jake thought I was headed toward.

Jimmy didn't budge. "And you're the one she flipped out on. Ah, is that what this is about? Are you two trying to use me to mend some old rift?"

For an obnoxious ass, he was surprisingly astute, but I was not about to give Jake a chance to answer. No way was I giving this dick the satisfaction of seeing us argue. Plus, as annoying as he was, I now felt a personal investment in getting him back on track. If there was hope for someone this far gone, surely there was hope for me.

"You got it. Out of bed with you."

"Why?" He sounded like a small, bratty child.

"We have a plane to catch," Jake chimed in.

"Fuck no we don't. I don't fly."

"That's why we're here, remember? What do you need? A sedative?"

"I'm not coming." As Jimmy crossed his arms and pouted, Jake crossed the room in three long steps.

"Yes, you are. That was the deal, man." He strained to hoist Danger from the bed, as the decrepit rockstar wriggled away from his grip.

"Get your paws off me. Get out of my house." Danger reached for a glass perched precariously on the head of his bed and took a swig. His eyes looked clearer when he finally lowered it.

"You said if we got you a show in California, you'd give us the *Happy Skalidays* files," I said, trying to play good cop. "You want to do a show in California, right?" It really was like talking to a child.

He took another sip and tipped his head to the side. "Why do you want those files so badly? You don't care about the others?"

"The others are online," Jake said.

"Shit, they are?" Jimmy stood, wobbling slightly. "I thought I took them all down. Fucking corporations, taking money for my art, giving me nothing, giving it all to politicians and shit." He took a step toward a computer tower in the far corner. "I'll delete them all—that'll show 'em. Might as well get rid of the originals too. Fuck ton of good they've done me."

"No!" Jake and I shouted in unison, moving as one to grab Danger. With Jake's arms wrapped around Jimmy's chest, and mine encircling his waist, our arms touched and our eyes met. Jake offered a small smile, which I returned before the smell ruined the moment. Danger's stench was so overwhelming it took effort not to cough.

It did not take much effort, however, to wrestle him to the bed. He put up a much smaller struggle than he had when Jake had tried to lift him out of it, and once we'd succeeded, he went limp, lying back against the crumpled sheets and sighing as we both towered over him to make sure he didn't make a break for the computer again.

"Come on. We have to go." Jake looked at his watch.

Jimmy shook his head from side to side, eyes closed. "It was a pipe dream. A Hail Mary. I don't know why I thought anyone would want to see me in California if they don't want to see me in New York. Fucking get on a fucking airplane and be fucking miserable and then no one fucking comes. No thank you." He sounded close to tears.

I got it. I totally got it. I knew what it was like to pour your heart into something and then wonder what the point had been. I'd never imagined successful musicians might feel that way, too. I hoped this whole thing was worth the hassle.

"No." Jake's voice was kinder. "The show's all planned. A bunch of people are coming."

Danger opened his eyes. "Really?"

Jake nodded earnestly. Was this true? I hadn't done anything to plan or promote the show, since I'd assumed it was no longer happening, but I played along.

"Yeah, it'll be huge. People are stoked." I reminded myself it was a lie—a way to get Danger on the plane. Apparently, Jake had figured out basic logistics on his own, but I couldn't get my hopes up for something actually fun or cathartic. Still, I couldn't stop the tiny flutter of optimism when I pictured a full house, the first real ska show I'd been to in ages.

"Well, shit, man, why didn't you say so?" Danger's demeanor changed instantly, and he sat up and downed the rest of the warm contents from his glass.

"But we've got to go," Jake said, with another glance at his watch. "The plane leaves soon. Get your stuff. Get whatever you need."

"I think he needs a shower." I avoided eye contact with the aging singer. "I don't think they'll let him on the plane like this."

Jake looked Danger up and down. "Make it quick. Brush your teeth, too."

$$\star^\star_\star \star^\star_\star \quad \star \star \quad \star^\star_\star \star^\star_\star$$

CHAPTER 23: JAKE

The shower helped, but dude was still a shadow of his former self. It was hard to believe this was really the guy who had intimidated me so much as a teenager I'd been afraid to talk to him.

We reached the gate right as the airline employee called our group to board.

"Thank you, Mr. Weiner." She handed Jimmy's boarding pass back with a smile.

"What did you...?" he started to ask, but I took his shoulders and led him down the jetway.

"It's your name, bud. Let it go."

"We're not in first class?" he asked as we found our row.

"Dude." I was already beyond tired of dealing with him. "Sit."

"Maybe we should put him in the middle," Sailor suggested, and I nodded. Maybe my body mass would muffle his kvetching.

"I wanted the middle anyway." Jimmy sounded like the child he was.

I helped Jimmy lift his bag and guitar case to the overhead compartment, and we all settled in. "I'm surprised you don't need help buckling," I mumbled as we snapped our seatbelts closed and the flight attendant closed the aircraft door.

"Oh boy," Jimmy said. "Oh boy." I looked at the singer, who was beginning to shake. He really was afraid of flying. "Oh fuck."

I tried to shush him. "There are kids." In the row across from us, a mother nursing a baby glared, and a second little face peeked out from behind her.

"Oh fuck," Jimmy said louder as the plane rumbled to life and began backing away from the terminal. "Fuck me."

I looked to Sailor, but she looked as clueless as I felt about what to do.

"Get me fucking off of here," Jimmy said, his panic rising. He made to unbuckle his seatbelt, but I grabbed his hand. I'd let my mom dictate my decisions in high school, then I'd let Hillary run my life. I wasn't about to let this asshole walk all over me. Sailor grabbed his other arm as he turned to me with wide eyes. It was hard not to have some sympathy for the guy.

"It's ok, dude, really," I said. "You've got this. You're Jimmy Danger!"

He gripped my hand tighter and nodded. "Ok. Ok. It's ok. Cool." But as the plane began moving down the runway, picking up speed, he started to flail. "No, no, no. Get me off of here." Sailor moved her grip from his arm to his other hand, and he squeezed us both hard, his knuckles white. He held on as the plane took off, rumbling its way into the atmosphere, and he didn't loosen his grip until the fasten seat belt sign dinged off.

Finally, a flight attendant made her way down the narrow aisle and asked if we'd like a drink.

"Water, please," Sailor said.

"Me, too."

"I'll take a vodka neat," Jimmy said. "And I'd take a drink of you, too." He eyed the back of her skirt as she walked away. Sailor rolled her eyes.

"Not cool, dude," I said. "You can't talk to women like that." But I could see he was still tense, his eyes still darting back and forth. How much of his whole schtick was a defense mechanism? Out the window, the sun was setting.

The attendant returned with our drinks, and we pulled out our tray tables for our cups. She handed them to us as the captain came over the intercom. "Good evening ladies and gentlemen. It's a lovely night to fly, the sky is clear, and we hope to have you to Ontario, California in...let's see...four hours and thirty seven minutes. I want to wish anyone celebrating tonight a very happy sixth night of Hannukah."

Looking around, I saw several men on the flight wore yarmulkas.

The little boy across from us grinned up at his mother. "We celebrate Hannukah!"

"It's a great night to celebrate, because our westward itinerary means we'll spend most of the flight at sundown," the captain continued. "If you'll bring your attention to the front of the aircraft, our wonderful flight attendant, Jared, who has fifteen years of service with us, by the way—thank you, Jared— has an electric menorah. We welcome you to recite the blessings with us as he lights it."

At the front of the plane, Jared pulled a small electric menorah from a shelf and switched on the lights, one by one. As the plastic candles flickered, something shifted inside me. Never in my life had I been somewhere public where Judaism was not an anomaly. Temple didn't count. There, it was still like the knowledge of being outsiders in our town hung over everyone.

I thought of all the Christmas parties in school, all the Easter bunnies at the mall, the "Merry Christmas"es from store clerks. They'd never upset me, but I'd also never acknowledged how left out I'd felt—how much it probably contributed to my loneliness—until right now, when I felt so included. Was this what it felt like to be part of a community? Like who you were was worthy of celebration?

My voice cracked as I said the blessings before it blended with the low hum of many other passengers. On the other side of Jimmy, Sailor said them, too. And between us, Jimmy had relaxed, his body looser, his eyes almost closed. I looked at his lips and saw he was mouthing the words, too. By the end of the prayer, he was out.

Sailor looked at the sleeping singer and then back to me. She, too, seemed subdued—more relaxed, less angry. "His hair is almost as embarrassing as yours in your bar mitzvah pictures." She smirked, but my shoulders tensed. Noticing, her smirk morphed into a frown. "What's wrong?"

"Nothing."

"It doesn't look like nothing."

I was too tired to play this guessing game, and way too tired to think of a snarky response. I leaned forward and rested my head on the tray table. "I'm not in the mood to be made fun of." I really wasn't. As I breathed in, the plastic hard on my forehead, I remembered we still hadn't eaten anything since breakfast. My tooth was aching, too. The adrenaline of getting Jimmy out the door, to the airport, and into the sky was wearing off, and I was exhausted, hungry, and miserable.

Sailor's brow creased. "I was joking. I love your bar mitzvah pictures. They're amazing."

"You make fun of me constantly. I'm over it."

"That's what we do. We tease. I didn't know it hurt your feelings."

I sat up. "No, it's what *you* do. I tease you playfully, but you mock me constantly. You think it's funny, but it's not funny when it's constant. It starts to feel like you aren't joking. You have never shown me you actually like me—all of me."

"I'm not a mindreader, Jake. I didn't know—" She stopped mid-sentence, as we both realized the irony. "I'm sorry. I thought it was our thing. I never meant to make you feel bad about yourself. I should have paid closer attention to how you reacted."

I sighed and fought back tears. "I'm sorry, too. I should have thought more about why you were so intent on staying. Or at least tried to talk to you more about it."

"I can't leave her." Sailor's voice cracked as she wiped her cheeks with the back of her hands, which she'd pulled her hoodie down to cover. "She's totally in her own world. You know that." I did. Rainbow had always been a character, but I didn't know how much it weighed on Sailor. "But I guess you don't know the extent of it. I make sure she pays her bills. When she needs someone to repair something I make the calls for her. I remind her about daylight savings."

"You're right. I didn't know." I reached across Jimmy to put my hand on Sailor's knee. It was incredibly awkward, stretching across the seat between us, my arm hairs bristling at contact with the passed out singer, but I needed to touch her—needed to let her know I was here, and that I heard her.

"But mostly, I can't leave her alone. She doesn't have any friends. The neighbors all think she's a weirdo. And my dad..." She trailed off.

"You're all she has," I finished. Sailor nodded. "I know the feeling. When it comes down to it, I probably couldn't be this far from my mom either. Even visits to Sacramento were tough, knowing she was by herself."

Sailor nodded again. "That must have been hard."

"Honestly, it's probably why I always dream about leaving. Because in reality, it's impossible. Gotta rebel somehow, you know? No one wants their mom to have so much hold on them."

"You know," Sailor said. "It's probably why I'm so stubborn about music. I have to prove to myself being stuck is good. I have to justify it somehow because I know the idea of only staying to take care of my mom is depressing. But fuck SoCal." She was smiling, though she was still sniffling a bit. "And fuck overbearing moms."

"No way," I said. "Fuck New York. New York is stupid and boring and cold."

Sailor's smile widened so I continued.

"Fuck the subway, fuck good bagels. Fuck it all. Southern California is where it's at."

Sailor snorted, her eyes still wet.

"Seriously. I would have stayed for you. I like Southern California." It was true—I loved being close to the beach and the mountains and the year-round nice weather, but that wasn't what would have kept me there. "If my mom wouldn't have killed me for turning down Berkeley, I wouldn't have cared about dealing with her all the time. I would have stayed for you in a heartbeat." I kept my arm stretched across Jimmy Danger even as my fingers tingled from the awkward angle, holding on to Sailor's knee as the plane sailed on through the everlasting sunset.

F**rom:** Tony Danger

      Sent: April 19, 2013 3:15 PM

To: Jesse Diaz-Ortega

Subject: Re: Re: Summer/Fall Opener

I wanted to talk one on one. Jimmy's been getting a little out of hand. Call me when you can.

***

From: Jesse Diaz-Ortega <>

      Sent: April 19, 2013 6:47 PM

To: Tony Danger <>

Subject: Re: Re: Summer/Fall Opener

I'm sure he'll be fine, Tony. He's a rock star.

CHAPTER 24: SAILOR

"Dude, can you not put your feet on the couch?" Jake said. Jimmy Danger huffed and placed his boots back on the floor, slumping so low only his head rested against the back pillow. How was this man almost 40?

I was tempted to ask Jake if he wanted me to stay over so he didn't have to be alone with him, but I didn't want to be presumptuous.

I was still trying to figure out where Jake and I stood. We had apologized, sure, but things were still weird. I knew neither of us wanted to do this back and forth game. It was exhausting and heartbreaking, not to mention awkward. He had held onto my knee on the plane until Jimmy woke up hyperventilating during landing, but we hadn't touched since. How could we go from fighting to ok? What were the steps in between?

"This pizza is disgusting." Danger kicked the box until the corner protruded over the edge of the coffee table.

"We know. It's barely pizza. You'd prefer a pie from a New York dumpster," I said. We know."

We'd been beyond starving when we got back, and pizza had been the quickest option to feed all three of us cheaply. He hadn't stopped talking about it since—no thank you, but multiple comments about how he could make a better pizza with his taint.

I could suggest Jimmy stay at my place—at least Roger was there to buffer—but if he treated our place like he was treating Jake's, Roger might murder the guy before the show.

Jake interrupted my deliberations. "Sailor and I have to go get some things ready for the show. Do you want me to put on the TV? I don't have any kid channels, but I'm sure I could find something."

Jimmy growled. "Fuck off."

Jake yawned. "Don't touch anything, ok?"

Jimmy nodded as he kicked his legs back up onto the couch.

"Shoes." Jake glared.

"Alright, alright." Jimmy let one foot, then the other, fall dramatically to the floor.

"What do we need to do?" I asked, once we were settled in Jake's car. He didn't turn it on, just leaned back against the head rest and closed his eyes, sighing in relief.

"Nothing. I just had to get away from that guy."

"Fair."

Jake opened his eyes. "We could go to your place?"

I wasn't going to object.

Roger was home with Desmond when we arrived, the former back to sitting cross-legged in the middle of his clothes pile, and the latter snorfling as she gobbled kibble.

Roger looked up to see me and Jake. "Well, hello. How was New York?"

"Meh," I said, and Jake and I laughed.

"You didn't get the rockstar?"

"Oh we did," Jake said. "He's a nightmare. We left him at my place."

"This sounds like a story. You'll have to fill me in later."

It really had been. It had been less than 48 hours there and back, but somehow the trip felt like a whole separate lifetime. Maybe, I thought, this is what I'd missed out on staying rooted here. Maybe people took vacations, moved across the state or the country, because time moved differently when you moved spaces too.

"Please tell me you didn't help my mom with her toilet." I hoped I hadn't pawned her off with my refusal to deal.

On the other hand, an image of still-running water made my chest tighten—what would her water bill be? Was I going to have to spend hours on the phone with the utilities company pleading senility on Rainbow's behalf and begging them to forgive the debt because I'd refused to make a five minute phone call from New York? Still, I was proud I had set a boundary and stuck with it.

"I didn't know Rainbow had a toilet that needed help. I've been chilling with Desmond and trying to get rid of all the shit I've accumulated over the last ten years. Please tell me why I saved the receipts from every pair of shoes I've ever purchased. Or all of my DVDs. We don't even have a DVD player anymore."

At her name, Desmond abandoned her bowl and scampered over, and I bent to pet her, but the pup brushed right past me and began jumping at Jake, resting her paws on his knees.

"Hey, buddy." Jake knelt down and scratched behind her ears. Desmond wagged her stump of a tail and tried to worm onto his lap, and Jake had to put a hand on the floor to avoid tumbling over. "Whoa!" He laughed.

"She likes you," I said. The grin on Jake's face was almost as adorable as the Frenchie's sloppy kisses.

"And I like her! Don't I, buddy? Don't I like you?" He was speaking in a baby voice, his nose rubbing Desmond's, the dog nearly frantic with affection, drool hanging from her open mouth in a long line. Was this how other women felt seeing a man hold a baby?

"Ahem." Roger stood and cleared his throat. "I'll be in my room. Don't mind me. Lots of packing to do. I'll be in there for..." He looked at his vintage silver watch—a favorite thrift store find. "A long, long time. With my headphones on. Come on, Des."

My face grew hot as Roger and Desmond disappeared into the master suite, but Jake tilted his head back and to the left, laughing. Maybe I wasn't being presumptuous after all. I grew redder as I remembered the last time we had "alone time." Repaying my orgasm debt certainly wouldn't be the worst way to move past this awkward post-apology/pre-official-feelings-talk stage. The warmth moved from my face to my throat and settled somewhere in my lower belly. But something was still off. I wanted to fool around, but I still wanted to clear the air first.

"I'm sorry," I blurted. "All you've done is go out of your way to be sweet and generous. I should never have been an asshole. You're responsible and mature and you were doing what you needed to do and I did like New York. I loved New York, I just couldn't..."

"I hate my job," Jake interrupted. "It's stupid and meaningless and not fulfilling and I'm totally a pawn for the man."

We both laughed.

"I won't call you a sellout. I'm trying to stop teasing. But your job does sound boring as hell." I paused. "But I should do something that doesn't make me so dependent on Roger. Obviously." I looked around. "Thank God he's leaving the furniture or this place would be close to empty when he leaves."

"I'm sorry, too. I love how you refuse to compromise yourself for anyone. Even if it is mainly a way to justify having to stay, I love how you love your wacky mom and how you sacrifice so much for her. You're definitely more mature than I am in that sense."

"Obviously," I deadpanned, then halted. "Shit, sorry. I hope that didn't hurt your feelings. I'm trying to pay more attention but it's a habit to—"

"Shh." Jake brought a finger to his lips. "I do understand sarcasm. You're good. Sorry if I made you self conscious about—"

I stood on my tiptoes and kissed him, sick of the apologizing from both of us. I'd already forgiven him—all I'd needed was the segue. Tripping over each other again, neither of us willing to separate, I felt the Pauline Black photo underfoot as we found our way to the bed.

There, Jake lowered me onto my back. Looking up at him, the tenderness in his eyes, I relaxed onto my checkerboard comforter, letting its warmth envelop me, and pulled him down close. We kissed and kissed and I lost myself in my senses—the weight and heat of Jake and the blanket, the shimmering stars behind my closed eyes. Even the smell of days of travel on Jake was sweet—a reminder of the miles we had walked side by side.

After what seemed like forever, I reached under Jake to shimmy out of my black tights, then kicked, tossing them to the floor.

Jake wasted no time reaching under my skirt. His fingertips pressed at my lower hip, then higher, before he ran his whole hand down my side from waist to thigh.

"That tickles," I laughed into his neck. Tickling was vulnerable and silly and intimate—I'd avoided it in my previous hookups, preferring to get down to business, but now I let Jake linger, running his fingers up and down, pausing each time he found a spot that made my skin contract.

"Are you not wearing underwear?"

"I never do with tights. It's uncomfortable."

Jake closed his eyes, looking almost exasperated. "Oh my God, that's so hot. Now I'm going to get hard every time I see you in tights."

"Good." I was breathless, desperate for him to touch me like he had the other day, and he did, exploring with his fingers, moving in an arc from hips to midline, then trailing downward from my bellybutton. He traced a line where panties would have been, making slow circles, like a massage, teasing.

If this continued much longer, I would have to put his hand where I wanted it. Finally, like he could sense I was losing patience, Jake slipped a finger inside, sending warmth across my abdomen from hip to hip.

"Mmmm," I moaned, and bucked against him, feeling his erection pressing through his jeans.

"Fucckkkkk," he groaned.

In a flash, I remembered last time, when Jake had been the sole provider of pleasure, and as amazing as his fingers felt, I wanted to make him feel good, too.

"Take off your pants," I said, and Jake didn't argue.

He got to his knees and unbuttoned his jeans, throwing them to the floor before the words were all the way out of my mouth, and forcing me to bite back a comment about Houdini.

Maybe I did need to work on thinking before I spoke. With most people, my mean comments were a defense mechanism, but with Jake, I thought they'd been a mutual joke. If he wasn't in on it, though, it wasn't fair to subject him to the cynicism I held for most of the world.

Getting up on my own knees, I took Jake's hips in my hands and looked at him, his green plaid boxers at eye level. The tip of his erection peeked out of the top, from behind the elastic waistband, already a drop of pre-come leaking from its end. I eyed it hungrily.

I wanted him in my mouth, all of him.

I wanted him to fill it—to make him moan in pleasure and to feel the hum of it through my own teeth. I didn't just want him to come. I wanted to make him come so hard he got lost in it, the way he had done for me.

Before I could wrap my lips around Jake, though, a faint rose fragrance pricked my nostrils. I giggled, recognizing the scent instantly.

Jake turned his head toward the door. "Do you smell something?"

"It's one of Roger's artisan candles. The one he lights when he's feeling both romantic and nostalgic. He usually burns it when he's rewatching *The Real World: Portland.*"

Jake laughed, but I had to admit the fragrance evoked a reaction. I refused to watch reality television with Roger, but the era of that particular season hadn't evaded me. My friend had conditioned me. The combination of rose, smoke, and wax brought me instantly to 2013.

Growing serious again, I lowered Jake's boxers to his thighs and he shivered as his hard-on flexed. Resting my palms on the bed I leaned closer and brought him into my mouth, slowly, letting my jaw relax as I tasted the length of him.

"Jesus," Jake moaned. Up and down I slid, slowly taking him in until the head touched the back of my palate, then gliding back up and running my tongue along the ridge.

Jake's hips stayed perfectly still, his only movements the rapidly increasing rise and fall of his chest and the rhythmic swelling of his hard-on each time I took him in. A low, steady groan hummed from his throat.

Suddenly, I felt his hand on the back of my head, his fingers intertwining with my hair. "I want to fuck you," he said. "Please, can I fuck you?"

And though I'd wanted to be selfless, though I'd wanted to be giving, there was no way I could say no to that. I wanted it too. I really, really wanted it.

I lifted my head to meet Jake's eyes. "Yes."

"My God, you're beautiful. I can not even tell you how many times I have imagined this exact moment."

I rested back onto my knees and from there, Jake helped me move to my back. Again, he towered over me, his head drawing closer to kiss me softly at first, then harder. I relaxed, relieved to let him take control again.

"Do you have a condom?" he whispered into my ear.

"Fuck. No." Dammit. I needed him inside me.

Frustrated, I sat up, ready to break the mood to drive to the the drug store down the street. But before I could muster the will to leave the bed, I saw that on the floor of my bedroom was a small silver foil square, about a foot from the door, as if someone had slipped it under.

"Oh my God. Roger is ridiculous." I laughed, nodding my head toward the condom on the floor.

"But a godsend," Jake said. "Thank you!" he called out, and we both laughed.

Our giggles soon turned to panting breaths as we resumed making out, my hands fumbling over Jake's shoulders and hairy chest, Jake struggling to keep kissing me as he rolled the condom on.

"Are you ready?" he asked, once he'd managed it, and I shook my head enthusiastically in the affirmative. I was more than ready. We took a shared breath. It felt so, so good.

My body opened to him, the sensations of fullness spreading all through my belly.

"It's so good." I was embarrassed by how obvious the statement sounded aloud.

Jake laughed, breathily, as he moved slowly in and out. "I'm gonna come if you keep saying that."

I lifted my hips to meet him. "Good." I wanted that—I wanted him to feel what he'd made me feel. As he slowed down further, squeezing his eyes tight for a moment, frozen as if willing himself not to finish yet, I was thankful. I wanted to enjoy this longer.

Jake opened his eyes cautiously, and then, balancing on one arm, reached the other down to find me with his fingers. As he continued to move slowly inside me, pausing every few thrusts to take a deep breath, he rubbed circles of matching speed, right in the perfect spot.

My climax built slowly, thanks to Jake's patience, and when it surfaced, it lasted for what felt like minutes. It was not the usual, frenzied rush to a buzzing orgasm I was accustomed to, but a steady climb, til my whole body lifted in a tight sustained pleasure, one that hinted at release, then continued, began to relax, then persisted, for what felt like a very long time.

My clenching climax was apparently too much for Jake, and he, too, came—hard, from the looks of it, his face almost pleading, his mouth agape.

After, once Jake had tied off the condom and thrown it in the black and white checkered plastic trash can by my desk, we lay cross-wise on my bed, so that our legs dangled off the side. I kicked mine back and forth while Jake stared up at the glow in the dark stars on my ceiling, breathing slowly.

"I'm so happy we lost that album," he said finally.

"Me too." I rolled over and buried my face in his chest.

"I never thought Jimmy Danger would help me get laid."

His t-shirt muffled my laugh, sending my warm breath back to me as I closed my eyes.

CHAPTER 25: JAKE

I hoped Sailor hadn't thought I'd suggested her place because I'd wanted to hook up. I mean, obviously it had crossed my mind, but it wasn't the *only* reason. I'd told the rest of the band we would practice here since it would have been impossible to move Sailor's drums without an explanation, and Jimmy had provided an annoying, but convenient, excuse to leave my house. Sure, I'd originally planned to sleep in my own bed and make my way here in the morning, but I wasn't going to complain.

Blinking awake, I took in the decor of her bedroom for the first time. CD liner notes were stapled to walls, still creased in the center. There was checkerboard everywhere. I was jealous. I could have decorated like this, but I'd never had the chance to design my own space. As a kid, I'd been stuck with the sports theme, and then in college, my roommate's gaming chair had taken up half the space, and he had insisted on decorating the rest with classic dorm decor—lava lamps, MC Escher posters, a bong. After, Hillary had convinced me her neutral colors and cheesy word art were adult, but who was she to decide what adult meant? Maybe I wouldn't make all the same choices as Sailor, but at least her room had character. If we decorated together, there was definitely a middle ground—we could put flyers and posters in frames, maybe one checkerboard accent wall.

But I was getting ahead of myself.

I looked at my watch. The rest of the band was scheduled to arrive any minute and I had to find a way to get us up and dressed. Sailor probably wouldn't be thrilled if I sprang a reunion on her before she'd brushed her teeth. Shit. Last night had been amazing, and I'd slept like a brick, but now the prospect of moving from Sailor's bed was torture. Her head fit so perfectly into the dip of my chest, and I didn't want to give her the impression I thought lying here was anything other than heaven.

I could tell her why we had to get up, but I didn't want to ruin the surprise. I wanted the epic moment when she realized what was happening.

I faked a yawn and felt Sailor's head rise with my chest. "Should we...?" I lifted onto my elbows and Sailor sat up, as confused as I would have been if she'd initiated the end of cuddling.

"I don't want to move. Can we stay here all day? Or forever?"

God, did I want to.

"My mouth tastes gross," I said. It wasn't a lie. "I'm gonna borrow some tooth-paste and brush with my finger, if it's ok."

"Sure." She motioned toward the bathroom. "Toothpaste is in the second drawer."

"Do you want to, too?" I realized how weird the question was immediately.

"Brush my teeth?" Sailor's hand shot up to cover her mouth. "God, is my morning breath that bad?"

"No! Not at all. Just wondering if you wanted to start the day. I'm excited to hang."

"Oh...kay." Sailor followed me.

I tried not to wince as we stood side by side in front of the mirror, her with a red sparkly toothbrush, me with my index finger in my mouth, my loose tooth screaming each time I got close.

Focus on her, I told myself, and it helped. Looking at Sailor's reflection, her hair tousled, still in the jogger sweats and grey tee she'd put on last night to sleep in, I couldn't believe how lucky I was.

Back in her bedroom, Sailor lazily pulled some tights over her long legs as I got back into the clothes I'd been wearing for two days—some 15,000 steps, and two airplane rides—and tried not to stare at her bare ass under the sheer fabric.

Out in the living area, Roger sat on the couch in his old rude boy attire, tapping his legs and staring at the door. We exchanged a quick glance. *She doesn't know yet,* I attempted to convey with my eyes. Apparently he got the message because he stilled his fidgeting and plastered a casual smile onto his face.

"You kids have fun last night?"

"Ew, Roger," Sailor said. "Why are you dressed up? Should we get some lunch or something? We don't have a ton of groceries right—"

The doorbell rang, interrupting whatever Sailor was going to say. It opened before I could stand back up and Sonia stepped in, Go and Romero close behind.

Sailor looked at me, her eyes wide. "No."

"Yes," I said, and before she even said hello to our old bandmates, she grabbed me and kissed me, making my cheek ache again. Roger stood, his posture loose now the secret he'd been holding was out, and grabbed his trumpet from behind a couch cushion.

"For you, babygirl. We're opening for Danger." He looked at Sailor, who was crying.

"You two." She shook her head. "It's too much." She went to Roger, squeezing him tightly as he lifted her from the floor with his free hand and spun her around. When she came back to me, I dipped her, almost throwing my back out with my attempt at a swoon-worthy kiss.

"Oof." I pulled us both upright. My arm still tight around Sailor's waist, I turned to Sonia, Romero, and Go. "Hey guys!" Beside me, Sailor was beaming. It was every bit as epic as I'd hoped.

"Wooooo-ooo." Go cheered like the audience track to a cheesy sitcom. "Didn't know this was porno practice." Apparently Danger wasn't the only one who hadn't grown up.

"Dude," I said in warning. I wasn't about to let anyone's misogyny ruin this moment.

"Sorry, sorry." Go put his hands up in surrender. "But for real—you two smashed yet?"

"God da—," I started, but my cursing was interrupted by the sound of a comedy rimshot.

"See?" Go motioned toward Sailor. "Your girl thinks I'm funny."

"Kidding," Sailor said. "You're a goon."

Go pantomimed swishing a basketball. "Go-go-go-Goon!"

From the corner of the room, Desmond let out a small yelp. She was nervous about all the new people, all the noise, I realized. My heart seized. I related to that dog. I was nervous, too, even under the crazy happiness.

"I better put her out." Roger took the dog by the collar, and I gave the pup a farewell pat on the flank as they passed, Roger leading her to the sliding glass door to the backyard. What was it Hillary always posted along with cute pictures of babies? Her ovaries were aching? Whatever the male equivalent of ovaries was, they ached as I watched the dog's stubby legs trot outside.

Roger returned a moment later. "I'll take lead vocals." He said it matter of factly, leaving no room for discussion about Hillary's absence.

We were rusty at first—it was clear Sailor had been the only one to practice consistently, and Roger was particularly uncomfortable singing the lead parts, but soon we reached a version of our old chemistry. It was palpable, when the room shifted and everything clicked. Looking around, I could tell everyone else felt it too. It was a different world when we played together—one bigger than the sum of its parts. How had I let myself forget this world existed?

I had never intended to lose it when I went to Berkeley. I thought it would follow me there, but somehow in the drama of my breakup with Sailor, then, once I was done moping, diving headfirst into a new relationship with Hillary, not to mention struggling to make my way at a place where I actually had to try academically, I had let it slip away.

Soon, I was lost in the music, and even my throbbing jaw was numb next to the happy buzzing in the rest of my body. I was still out of breath, for sure, but the discomfort was secondary to the high. I hadn't realized how much I'd missed this. It was different than just listening to music. We were *in* the music. It was a full body, immersive experience. If I was more Jewish I might compare it to a mikvah—it was like bathing in the sound.

Two hours later, we'd settled on the song we would play and agreed on a meeting time for the next day.

Sonia promised to get her coworkers to come out, and Go said his "boys" would spread the word.

"One more minute and I might have literally passed out," I said as I collapsed onto the couch.

"Dude, seriously," Romero said. "I need an epsom soak or something. I'll see you all soon."

"Wait!" Sonia called before her brother could move, and we all turned in her direction. "We need a selfie! Let's recreate the one from our old site." The suggestion brought a second wind to the group, and we all shuffled into position.

"Was Go next to me? Or Romero?" Roger asked.

"It was Romero. Go was over here," Sonia said.

"Next to Hillary," Go confirmed, and the room froze, everyone again unsure how to address the elephant in the room.

"Right." I was anxious to break the silence. "So stand next to me."

Finally, we were settled, our faces squeezed together, all older, some fuller, some thinner, but still us, and still glowing with the thrill of making music. Hillary was missing, but the group still felt whole. In high school, we had used Roger's phone for the selfie because it was better than the rest of ours, even though it didn't have a front facing camera. We'd had to do our best to all get into frame, and Roger had insisted on a dozen retakes. Now, though, we could see the photo as we took it—all our smiling faces preserved as a memory even as we lived it.

"Cuuuuute!" Sonia squealed as the shutter snapped and the image froze on screen.

"*You're* cute." Go winked at her.

"Fuck off, Go," Sonia said, as casually as she might tell someone "Gesundheit" or "Excuse me." "What are your Instagram names? I finally gave in and got the app but I'm not following anyone except some people from work and you, yet, Romero."

My mouth went dry. What if Hillary saw it? I'd hurt her plenty recently—what would she think if she found out we all got together and she hadn't been invited? She had always been self-conscious about fitting in with the rest of us, and this would be icing on the cake of our sudden breakup.

"ThatShipSailed," Sailor said.

"RudeRoger."

"HellBoy69," Go said.

"You don't have to tag me," I choked out.

"Come on," Sailor said. "The picture is great." I was touched by her reassurance—she had thought I didn't like the way I looked in the photo and instead of making a "you're not that fat" quip, she had been thoughtful and sincere.

I sighed. "ThatJewishJake." It would be fine. Sonia had said she only recently got Instagram. She was hardly following anyone. The probability of Hillary seeing the post, even if my tag upped it in the algorithm, was incredibly low.

Sonia smiled and began tapping at her phone, tagging each of us and speaking aloud as she wrote a caption. "Who remembers Skankin' Kiddos?" she read as she typed. "*Happy Skalidays* went missing. Whomp whomp. But we're bringing it back with a reunion show. We're older and better than ever. Catch us tomorrow at The Barn opening for THE Jimmy Danger. One song only! You don't wanna miss it!"

Suddenly, I was nauseous as another thought occurred to me. Hillary could be sensitive, but she also had a vindictive streak. She did sketchy stuff to undermine her work enemies all the time. What if being left out made her more than sad? She would understand the reunion had something to do with my feelings for Sailor. What if she was super pissed? What if she tried to do something about it? What if she tried to sabotage the show?

I forced a swallow. *No.* It was fine. Hillary wouldn't even see the post.

APRIL 18, 2013

JakeTheB@ndG33k: Thanks for the ride home last night, Hill

SaVedNSwEet: no worries. I know yours didn't work out

JakeTheB@ndG33k: understatement of the century

SaVedNSwEet: she doesn't deserve you, you know

JakeTheB@ndG33k: lol

SaVedNSwEet: it's true. If she expects you to give up your dreams for her unrealistic ones, she'd never be a good partner

JakeTheB@ndG33k: can we change the subject?

SaVedNSwEet: sure

JakeTheB@ndG33k: have you picked where you're going yet?

SaVedNSwEet: I got in to Stanford :D

JakeTheB@ndG33k: oh wow, congrats

SaVedNSwEet: thanks! I'm a little nervous about being so far from home. I'm glad you won't be super far though. I think it's only an hour to Berkeley :)

CHAPTER 26: SAILOR

"You gotta get up, man." Jake nudged Jimmy with the toe of his skate shoe.

"Why?"

"The show? The whole reason you're here? You faced your fears, dude. Don't let it be in vain."

Danger groaned. "I need a drink." Jake tugged him to his feet.

"Fine. We'll get you a drink. But let's go."

Elgin was waiting behind the counter when we arrived at The Barn, absorbed in scribbling into a ratty notebook.

Jake cleared his throat, and the bearded man lifted his head. "Welcome," he said. "I've been expecting you."

No shit he'd been expecting us. Jake had coordinated with him to plan the show.

"Well, here we are," I said.

"Aw, Master Danger." Elgin stepped around the bar and bowed to Jimmy. "At your service."

"Sweet, man. Can I have a beer?"

"My pleasure." Elgin disappeared and returned with a clear plastic cup of lager, which Jimmy downed in a single gulp before throwing the cup to the floor, shaking his head like a dog, and smacking his lips.

Elgin scurried on hands and knees to retrieve the discarded cup as Roger walked in the door and looked from the near-prostrating Barn employee still on all fours, to Jimmy, who, revitalized by the alcohol, was in the middle of a flying leap onto the stage. "What the ever loving queen of ska?"

Romero, Go, and Sonia arrived a moment later, as Elgin scrambled to his feet. "Shall we do a sound check?" he proposed.

Go guffawed and Roger rubbed his chin. "We...shall?"

Jimmy went first, tuning the guitar he'd brought for his solo set—checkerboard, of course, with a glittering silver strap—and repeating "test" into the mic as Elgin spun dials, adjusting the volume. My heart thumped against my ribs as I listened to Jimmy's amplified voice. It was only one word, but he was using his performance voice now, and my body's reaction to the familiar stimulus was visceral.

"Nah, man. Vocals forward," Jimmy said, and Elgin turned another knob. "That's it. That's it."

We were less picky about our levels. "Can you hear us all?" Jake called out. Roger hummed into the mic with uncertainty.

"Indeed, I can," Elgin confirmed.

"Then we're good."

From the wings, Jimmy shook his head. "Nah, bambinos. You need vocals. Better ones."

Roger rolled his eyes but didn't disagree.

"Feel free," Jake said. "Feel free to do anything helpful." Apparently the musician's sound check hadn't done as much to suppress his annoyance as it had for mine. So that only I could hear, he added, "I refuse to let this jackass ruin your day."

To everyone's surprise, Jimmy walked over to Roger and plucked the mic from his hand. I looked to Jake and our eyes widened. Roger, Sonia, Go, and Romero seemed equally unsure about what was happening.

"Do you want me to write down some lyrics or something?" Roger asked. "It's pretty simple but—" Elgin rushed forward and proffered his notebook.

Jimmy shook his head. "Let's go." He was bouncing up and down, shaking his head, pepping himself up.

"Uh..." I said. "Let's go, I guess."

Danger nodded.

Jake rolled his eyes. "This should be good."

With another shrug, I counted off, and we all watched in amazement as Jimmy Danger launched right into the vocals—our vocals, the ones we'd written over a decade ago and posted on our shitty website.

He didn't miss a word as his gruff, bedraggled facade melted away until he was the old Jimmy Danger—his face animated and his body in constant motion—a star, singing our song.

I should have been ecstatic—floored by this next layer of surprise and affirmation. Instead, my mouth felt dry, the thrill of the moment sucked out of the air like a vacuum. It felt off, and I couldn't place why. When Jimmy fled to the bathroom after the sound check, I followed, waiting outside the door until he emerged. When he finally did, I crossed my arms. "How'd you know our lyrics?"

Danger shrugged, then patted my cheek with a wet hand. "Oops. Forgot to wash."

I cringed at the clammy fingerprints he left behind. "God you're worse than Go." I turned around. I wasn't sure what I'd been hoping to learn by following him, and whatever it was, he wasn't going to give it to me.

"Hey, I was kidding. It's water." I started walking as he called after me. "Hey, wait."

I paused but didn't turn back around.

"I meant it when I complimented you kids back then. I really liked your music. Still do."

My steps slowed, along with my breathing.

Jimmy continued speaking to my back. "I looked it up when we got back from tour. Printed out the lyrics. Downloaded the songs."

There was no hint of his usual ribbing tone.

"They're pretty etched on my heart, Sailor. I listened to your band...a lot...during a pretty tough time in my life."

I swiveled to face him and for a moment I didn't speak—just studied his features. They were softer, and older, like he'd given up his fight against time all at once.

"When your band broke up?" I asked.

There it was—out in the open, and though I suddenly understood why his singing our song had felt so ominous, I still didn't know if I wanted to hear his answer. If Jimmy Danger and I had been moping and listening to each others' music while we mourned the loss of our respective bands, it would prove beyond a doubt this washed up musician and I were as similar as I feared.

The parallel would be too perfect—our paths too pathetically intertwined. The location of this revelation— directly outside the same bathroom which had brought me and Jake back together—did not escape me.

This venue—this spot—was a pulsing star in the constellation of my destiny. It was like what Rainbow had told me about tarot cards—certain ones will bond to you, and you'll pull them over and over.

"Yes."

I winced.

"But that wasn't it. I..." Jimmy Danger looked at the ground as he paused. Finally, he met my eyes again. "You've probably noticed I...struggle."

I wanted to make a crack, but I stayed silent.

"With drugs. And alcohol. It's what broke Agents of Ska up."

I cocked my head. "SkaNews said it was interpersonal conflicts."

"I guess you could call it that. I was out of my mind on coke and I fucked up Anthony's car."

"Oh, shit." My limbs grew heavy as this new information registered.

Jimmy cleared his throat. "I only got worse after. Your music—you all and a few other bands—sometimes I think it's the only thing that kept me tethered to this side, ya know?"

I did know. I knew what it was like for music to be a lifeline. But I hadn't known, until this moment, what it was like to learn *your* music—your words and rhythms and melodies—had been a touchstone for someone else.

It all would have been worth it anyway, I thought—even if Jake and I hadn't come back to each other. If the brief time we spent making music together as kids had still made meaning like this for another person, it would have still been worth it.

"I've been on and off the wagon." He hadn't spoken so earnestly, so articulately, the entire trip, but now he was in full-on confession mode. "You could probably guess I was off when you found me. But you kids walked back into my life and dragged me back into the light. When I sang that song back there, something clicked. I realized it's time for a change. I'm grateful, Sailor."

Any remaining unease dissipated and I nodded, letting his words sink in.

"Now let's go play some ska." Jimmy straightened, and his features firmed again as he cupped me on the shoulder and guided me back toward the stage.

It wasn't long before a crowd started to arrive. I'd been skeptical about Jake's ability to get people out, especially since the college crowd was on winter break, but apparently he had known what he was doing. Soon the trickle of attendees became a stream, and as Elgin pulled the ropes to close the curtains—he'd dusted them, I observed—I was suddenly back in high school, my heart in my throat, waiting for the biggest moment of my life. My breathing was growing shallow when I felt hands on my deltoids, massaging them with the perfect amount of pressure, and I turned to see Jake behind me. Instantly, I relaxed, exhaled, and lowered my shoulders away from my ears.

"It will be perfect," he said.

"You said the same thing last time."

"And the show was perfect!"

"But after…" I trailed off.

He smiled and squeezed again. "We know better now. And I'm not going any-where."

I took a deep breath and nodded as the curtains opened again and, feeling slightly removed from my body, I jogged over to my drums.

"We're Skankin' Kiddos, and we have a special guest for you tonight!" Roger handed the mic to Jimmy, who ran out from the wings to decent applause. The cheers weren't as loud as I'd anticipated, and I could tell by the look in Jimmy's eyes he was disappointed, too, but the floor was packed, and that meant potential. Jimmy should know more than anyone that music could turn things around. Before he could pull any diva shit, I slammed my drum sticks together.

As I'd hoped, the crowd came alive immediately, though it was different than the last time we had played. This time, half the floor was a sea of cellphones held over heads, camera lights illuminated, the faces behind them watching the show on their screens. Jimmy didn't seem to mind though. He belted "Rude Empire" with all the enthusiasm of his former glory days. The crowd ate it up, and the phones lowered. When they did, I noticed the audience wasn't what I'd initially thought. There were the college kids I expected, but also—*also*—there were people our age and older—lines at the corners of their eyes, some with hair just starting to gray. And some of them had brought their kids—mini people decked out in checkers and teeny leather jackets, a boy in a Save Ferris hat, a girl with noise-canceling headphones and a shirt reading "No Naps til Brooklyn." They sat on shoulders and hips. One especially little one was asleep in their mother's arms. This was Sonia's baby, I registered, looking up from the bundled infant to see Sonia's wife Leila smiling back at me. My friend had made a human being, and she was here watching us play.

There were teenagers, too—fifteen or sixteen—beanies and baggy jeans. These kids had probably watched the Aquabats as toddlers, I realized. I had thought ska was dead, but it had just changed and grown.

As Roger's trumpet solo ended and Jimmy sang the final lyrics—"If my friends don't answer calls, I'll go meet them at the mall. Teach them how to skank real cool, start a band up at my school"—I wanted to hold on. I wasn't ready for this to be over. Looking at Jake, Hawaiian button up over his white t-shirt, face red with happiness and exhaustion, I segued into another round of the chorus. He had done this for me—for all of us. I'd been a brat at times, but Jake had still spent his time and money and emotional bandwidth on this moment. I could barely contain my adoration.

Soon, though I prolonged it as best I could, it was time for the crash out. I couldn't cling any longer. Summoning all the love straining at the walls of my heart, I closed my eyes and released it into a 15 second roll. Finally, forearms burning, I smashed the high hat, then the tom, then the cymbal, which echoed for a moment in the sudden silence. A second later, the crowd's screams were deafening, and my ears thrummed with the sound of their cheers as they morphed into a ringing white noise.

It took several moments to catch my breath. Then, as I set my sticks down, Jake appeared at my side, his grin enormous, and before I could say a word, he was lifting me from my stool, squeezing me so tightly that again, I could hardly breathe. "I love you," he shouted above the din.

"I love you, too," I said, and we kissed quickly before following our bandmates offstage. Jimmy remained on stage, staring out at the crowd and breathing heavily into the mic, as if he, too, were having an out of body experience. Slowly, the crowd quieted and the cell phones came back out as finally, Jimmy picked up his guitar from where it had been waiting at the back of the stage and draped the strap over his shoulder. From the pocket of his worn Dickies, he pulled a pair of dark secret agent glasses, and with a wink, put them on. Someone in the back of the crowd hooted, and Go shouted "Fuck yeah!" from the wings.

I could barely contain all my emotions. I had seen him standing right here a decade ago with those glasses. The sum of our collective experiences during the time since then was impossible to comprehend, but here we all were again.

"I'm Jimmy Danger. You may know me from Agents of Ska, and I'm here to play a few old bangers," he said, before launching into a one man version of "Horn to Be Wild."

"Weird choice," Romero said. "To play this without a horn." The crowd seemed to concur as they continued to bob their heads and cheer politely, the energy nothing like what it had been a moment ago. Jimmy noticed—his face falling was visible even behind the glasses.

"Uh oh," Jake said, and I braced myself for what was to come. I pictured Danger screaming at the crowd, throwing something across the room, smashing his guitar. Maybe it was this space—maybe The Barn had been built on the grave of some vengeful ska god committed to causing public freakouts.

But Jimmy didn't lash out. Instead, he paused mid-song and let his guitar hang loosely from its strap. He tucked the sunglasses back into his pocket. "Yeah, you're right," he said. "That sucked. Can I get the Kiddos back out?"

Jake and I looked at each other with mouths ajar. Did he mean...

"Yeah, come on out, you fuckers. They like you better."

We only hesitated a moment before running back to our spots. Instantly, the crowd erupted. "What are we playing?" I called to Jimmy, still not quite believing what was happening.

"Let's try 'Horn to Be Wild' again, now that we can play it like it's meant to be played."

Jake's face lit up and I nearly squealed with excitement for him. Roger was beaming too. This was the brass section's chance to shine, and it was so, so deserved. The song began, and again the venue was full of sound—not only the instruments, but the whoops and cheers of the audience, who jostled and collided as they tried to skank in the packed space.

As we played through a full set of Agents of Ska hits, I continued floating back and forth between dissociation—a sense of floating above myself, watching the scene play out like a memory—and intense presence and flow—my body and the music all that existed.

The music itself was rough. We hadn't practiced these songs, and we fumbled through several false endings, cracking up each time. At one point, Romero gave up and let his bass hang from his neck as he lifted his hands in surrender, making Sonia laugh so hard her sax honked.

But no one, on stage or off, minded the mess. The room sizzled with energy.

As the last song ended, I came fully back to my body an inch at a time, feeling first my hands, which still gripped my sticks, then my arms, which felt like jelly, then my feet, which I realized were still shaking with adrenaline. The last hour had been the culmination of every practice, every refused office job, every CD I'd held on to well past they started skipping.

Next to return was my vision, which, over the course of the last song, had narrowed to the periphery of my drum set. Suddenly, I was aware Jake was on his knees on the floor, his trombone beside him, a hand cradling his jaw.

"Fuck!" I shouted as I jumped up and ran to him. The crowd's enthusiasm had also shifted to confused muttering and pointing. Some took their phones back out to record. Worst case scenarios ripped through my brain as I imagined heart attacks and hospital beds. The world couldn't be so dark—could it?—to take Jake from me after the best moment of my life. "Are you ok? What happened?" I knelt beside him, frantically searching for any indication of what was happening.

"My tooth." His words were garbled. "Something's wrong." Relief flooded my body as I processed his answer—this wasn't life threatening—but he was still in pain.

"Let's go." I helped him to his feet. "Let's fix this."

CHAPTER 27: JAKE

"Sonia?" Sailor called, and a second later our saxophone player was at her side. "He says it's his mouth."

"Let's see." Sonia set her sax at her feet and took a step closer. "Can you open?"

I tried. Oof. "Yeah, that's pain. Stabbing pain."

"Sorry, bud." Sonia moved closer still. "Can you lift your chin up for me?" I obeyed. "Oh yeah, that's gotta hurt."

"What is it?" The worry in Sailor's voice pained me more than my mouth.

"It looks like you have an abscess by the loose tooth," Sonia said. "And your wire popped out of place so it's pressing against it. I'm surprised you haven't felt throbbing for days."

"I have." I looked at the floor, sheepish. "I thought it was the wire."

Sonia nodded. "Well, we need to get you in so the wire doesn't pop the abscess."

"What happens if it pops?"

"It will taste disgusting, for one. But it could spread infection and get pretty nasty. You'll want a doctor to fix the wire and drain the pus from the abscess with sterile tools." I was beginning to calculate emergency room costs when Sonia went on. "I'll call the office. She'll come in for emergencies, and since it's her work, she won't charge." That was a relief at least.

I was vaguely aware that a few feet away someone was scrambling onto the stage. Suddenly, a third face appeared to Sailor's left.

"Hillary." Fuck. Fuck fuck fuck. She had seen the post. She was here to make a scene, tell Sailor some horrible lie about me, inform me I owed her backpay for money she'd spent on silverware or something. In the attempt to prepare, I almost forgot the searing, pulsing pain in my mouth.

But Hillary's face was plastered with concern, her eyes wide and her chin trembling. "What happened?"

Sonia kept her eyes on me as she answered. "Tooth abscess. And a popped dental wire." Hillary's relief was visible. Sonia turned and smiled at her. "And hey, Hill. But we do need to get it taken care of." She took out her phone to call as Roger addressed the crowd on the mic. "Dental emergency, folks. All's good. You can go. Hope you enjoyed the show." Slowly, people trickled out, some lagging behind and still recording with their phones.

"You want to party?" Go asked Danger with a gentle shove to his arm. "You can stay with me."

"You know..." Jimmy looked thoughtful. "I don't think I do want to party."

I snorted, and immediately regretted it. "Ouch."

Jimmy glared at me. "Really."

I was skeptical, but Go shrugged. "You do you, man. I'm gonna scope out some college chicks. You coming, Romero?"

"No, dude. I'm going home to hang with my real-life girlfriend." He tipped his head toward the edge of the stage, where a hipster girl with fire engine red hair and blunt bangs smiled back at him.

"Boooooring."

"We've got weed," Romero said.

"And I'm in. You good, Jake?" Go asked.

"I'm good. Go get stoned. Have fun."

"Sweet. You coming, Hillary? Want to make it a double date?"

Hillary crinkled her nose. "As if."

"Take care of yourself, man," Romero said in my direction, before he jumped off the stage, Go behind him. The hipster girl hugged Romero, and the three of them took off together.

Roger moved his eyes briefly in Jimmy's direction. "I'll take this one back to the house. I have some last minute packing to do. I'll see you both soon, but call if you need anything."

"Thanks, Roger," I said. "For everything. Seriously, man, you're a real mensch. I owe you."

"You do. But you're welcome." He turned to Jimmy. "Let's go, queen." Amazingly, the singer followed without protest, whistling and swinging his arms.

Sonia returned as Sailor turned to Elgin, who had been observing the whole circus with palms pressed together in a prayer position. "Can we come back for our instruments later?"

"It would be my honor to guard them in your absence," Elgin said.

"Thanks," Sailor said. "We good to go?" Sonia nodded and Sailor reached for my hand, moving to push past Hillary, but my ex didn't budge. "Excuse us." Sailor's voice was clipped.

Hillary stepped aside to let us pass, but to my alarm, she followed right behind me, Sailor, and Sonia. She continued to follow us out of the building, down the sidewalk, and through the parking lot to Sailor's car, high heels clicking, and a large designer tote bouncing at her side. When Sonia opened the back door and got in, Hillary lifted her own foot to the floor of the car. Sonia paused for a moment before sliding across the back seat to let Hillary in after her.

"What are you—" I started, but Sailor hushed me, reaching across the center console to put a hand on my leg. Ok. Even if Hillary had come to ruin things with me and Sailor, it wouldn't work. We were in this together. Sailor gave me one more reassuring squeeze before starting the car. I looked her way and saw she was taking slow controlled breaths.

Rumbling out of Riverside, holding back yelps of pain at each pot hole and lane change, I tried to focus on Sailor beside me. She was so sexy and confident navigating the freeway, only glancing in the rearview mirror occasionally to see Hillary in the backseat, and doing her best to mask her scowl when she did.

Finally, we parked in front of the dark dental office.

"Can you rate your pain for me?" The dentist and Sonia led me through the dark office to the same room where I'd had the initial procedure. Hillary and Sailor walked on either side of me.

"8?"

Sailor reached for my hand, and on my other side, Hillary tensed.

The dentist's brow furrowed. "Not what I like to hear. Let's take a look."

As I settled onto the reclining treatment chair, Hillary and Sailor paused and eyed the one extra seat on the side of the room and then each other. Finally, Hillary tipped her head toward the chair, offering it to Sailor. Sailor sat, but looked up at Hillary with distrust. Then they both turned back to me as the dentist lowered a laughing gas mask to my nose. Their competing looks of sympathy were the last thing I remembered before the nitrous blurred my surroundings to stars and my thoughts grew light and fluffy, floating between them like clouds.

When my head cleared, the glaring brightness of the dentists' light was even more blinding in the otherwise dark office, and both women were still at my side, Hillary on the spare chair and Sailor squeezed next to my legs on the dentist chair. For a moment I wondered if I was hallucinating. Hell, maybe I had hallucinated the whole thing—the missing album, New York, The Barn—but Sailor squeezed my hand, and I knew instantly it was all real.

Sonia stood behind them, tapping away at the computer. Mentally, I surveyed my bodily sensations. My arms and legs were sore. My abs were, too. The show had been a workout, and I would probably be feeling it for days. My mouth, though, was mostly numb.

"Hey." Drool trickled down my chin. Sailor laughed and wiped it away.

"How are you?" she asked.

"You were incredible," I said. I could control my mouth with concentration. My thoughts were jumbled, and in my mind, I saw Sailor drumming, her face serene, her right arm reaching for the high hat, like a GIF on a loop. "You're always incredible."

She smiled. "*We* were incredible. But how are you feeling?"

With a glance at Hillary, I lowered my voice. "I feel like I love you," I whispered and watched as Sailor tried to suppress a smile. "I didn't whisper, did I? I tried to whisper."

Hillary rose to go. "I'm going to give you a minute."

"No—" Sailor moved to stop her. "You can—"

"No." Hillary placed a hand on Sailor's shoulder. "It's alright. Really." We both watched as she strode out of the room, the sound of her heels sharp on the hard floor, and I felt myself growing more lucid.

"I'll be back in a minute, too." Sonia said, and followed her out.

Sailor sat down again and looked at me. "I love you, too, Jake. I've always loved you. You know that."

My chest swelled, and I moved to sit up. I wanted to kiss her, but the quick change in position made me dizzy, so I laid my head back on the chair.

"We should live together," I said. "Since Roger's going and you need to figure something out."

"You're still out of it."

But I wasn't. My head was as clear on this as it had been on anything. "I'm not. I'm the opposite of out of it. I'm in of it. We should move in together. It makes sense."

Sailor shook her head. "I don't want to be your charity case."

"No...no! That's not what I meant. I want to live with you. At my mom's house if we needed to for awhile—I know you don't want to be with yours. Or I can move into your place. Anything. I want to be with you. To make a life with you."

"I don't know..." She looked pained. "I know my mom could use the extra help."

"There's a difference between helping your mom out and enabling her. She's the parent."

"Let's talk about it later."

"Ok." I didn't want to pressure her. Whatever made her happy—from now on, that's what I would do. "Whenever you're ready. But I do love you, Sailor."

"Even if I never grow up?"

"Don't grow up," I said. "Seriously. Don't fucking dare."

"What if I never get another drum student?"

"You can be my trophy wife and sit at home eating bonbons while I bring home the vegetarian bacon."

Sailor laughed, then grew serious again. "What if I don't want to get married? I mean, I might, someday, but..."

"Then you can be my trophy partner and sit at home eating bonbons." She laughed again. "But seriously. I don't need anything else. Just you. The real, whole you. I don't care if you don't know what you want. I want you. Even if you never have another drum student. Even if you never want to get married. Even if you never want kids. Even if you do want kids and then they hate ska."

"Can I kiss you?" There were tears in Sailor's eyes.

"You officially never have to ask. The answer is always yes."

"Even if you just had emergency dental surgery?"

"Oh. Right." I pointed to the non-injured half of my face. "Kiss this side."

Sailor leaned in for a gentle smooch. It was awkward, slightly numb, slightly painful, and I was suddenly unsure again if I was drooling, but in her kiss, I could picture all the ones to come—the painful and the perfect. "I love you," I said again.

"I love you too," Sailor said. Then, "Oh! Speaking of kids."

"You're pregnant?" I asked, half-joking, before realizing this was, in fact, a possibility. My heart started to beat hard. I had meant it—whatever Sailor wanted to do, whatever life choices she made, I was fully on board now, but still, the thought of it happening so soon...

"God, no. But we will have a baby. Desmond is staying with me."

My anxiety immediately transformed into excitement. "Desmond!" I paused. "But...Roger will be lost without her."

"He will be, I know. But we talked and even Roger agrees Desmond would be miserable in New York."

"Poor Roger." I couldn't focus on my sympathy for long. "But agh, this is amazing news. I can't wait to snuggle our floppy girl."

"Everyone clothed?" Sonia's voice called from the doorway.

"Yeah. Should we not be?" I asked. "Say the word and I'm naked."

Sonia laughed as she and Hillary returned, Sonia resuming her note taking and Hillary sitting beside me and Sailor again.

"Did I say anything embarrassing on the nitrous?"

"I promised not to tease you anymore." Sailor bit her lip, her eyes dancing.

"I made no such promises," Hillary said. "You said you wanted to watch *Kim Possible* because she was the voice of our generation. You went on for a long time about how much you identified with her as a kid and how you wish they had a *Kim Possible: All Grown Up* reboot to help you navigate adulthood."

I groaned, but Sonia shook her head. "I have heard so much worse. I'll be right back. Just need to get your release paperwork."

"So, I brought something for you." Hillary lifted her oversized leather tote bag onto her lap. "I came to the show thinking I could talk you out of it. Out of leaving." Suddenly, my heart began to race again, sweat pooling in the space behind my knees on the leather dentist chair.

"But I understand something now." Hillary reached into the bag and placed something into my hands.

I looked at the package and my racing heart stopped mid beat.. "Oh, shit...Hillary."

"Language," Hillary said.

There, in mint condition, was a copy of *Happy Skalidays*. It was fucking gorgeous—a full color picture of Agents of Ska in their heyday—before Jimmy Danger had fallen off the wagon; when Jerome Higgins, nonprofit director, was still nerdy Jerry Danger, all of them with Santa hats on and shiny red bows on their instruments. The plastic packaging was still on, a sticker from the record company still on the front.

"*Happy Skalidays*," Sailor and I said in unison.

"I thought I could win you over by being what you wanted. I've been trying to do it since we were kids. I joined the band to impress you. I went to Stanford to impress you. And I thought being the hero—bringing you the album, would impress you."

"Hillary," I started, but she wasn't finished.

"But I could never be who you wanted, like you could never really be who I wanted. I'm sick of trying to change us both."

The words hung in the air for several breaths.

"Thank you," I said finally. There was nothing else to say...except— "How did you—"

"I've had it since high school. I bought all their albums—I tried so hard to be as cool as Sailor, and I thought maybe if..." She trailed off. "They've been in my parents' spare room for years."

"Wow. Thank you. Really."

She looked from me to Sailor. "I'm happy for you. Both of you, really." She stood and moved for the door.

"Hillary," I called out, and she turned around, her hair swishing over her shoulder in a golden arc. "What should we do about the house? Sailor and I will probably..." I trailed off. Hill had been so generous—I didn't need to rub anything in. "I can't afford rent alongside mortgage payments."

"Don't worry about it," she said breezily. "I sold the other albums. Turns out mint condition records go for a lot. I'll be fine." She was gone before either of us could say another word.

Sailor and I stared at each other in disbelief for what felt like minutes until Sonia appeared again. "You're all set." She unhooked the bib from around my neck, raised the chair to a more upright position, and handed me several printed pages of aftercare instructions. "Try to take it easy, ok? You can ice your mouth, use gauze if you bleed, only soft food, no straws. The doctor wrote you a prescription for some painkillers, so take them as needed, but the discomfort should subside in the next couple days. Call us this time if it doesn't. Don't try to tough it out."

I nodded. "Deal."

"Oh," Sonia added. "No trombone. Give it a rest for a bit."

Damn. I was surprised at how disappointed those instructions made me. I wanted to keep playing—the night had reminded me why I loved it. But my disappointment only lasted a second before another feeling bubbled up in my chest. I would take a break from playing, but I would also come back to it. I was going to play music again regularly. My life was opening back up in so many ways. Suddenly a flash of insight from my twilight haze returned—we should incorporate klezmer into our style. The Jewish music would blend perfectly with ska and give us a super unique sound.

"Dude," I said, starting to tell Sailor my idea.

But Sonia spoke at the same time. "I think Hillary grabbed a rideshare, and the doctor said she can take me home, so you don't need to worry about me."

"A ride!" Sailor jumped up. "We have to get Jimmy and Roger to the airport."

CHAPTER 28: SAILOR

Roger opened the door and glared at us, one hand on his hip. "Well, look who it is. I really thought you were going to make me rideshare to the airport and let me leave without saying goodbye."

"Never." I smiled, but the smile quickly disappeared as the reality sunk in further that this was it. Roger was really leaving. I had somehow let myself forget how imminent it was amidst all the ups and downs of the last few days, and now it was right here at my feet.

Desmond trotted over and sniffed at Jake, who stood behind me, and Jake kneeled and fluffed her fur, rustling her head between his hands as he told her what a good girl she was and how he would take her on so many walks and give her so many treats. Roger watched, pleased, though I knew leaving Desmond was painful for him.

"Who's the bestest girl?" Jake asked, nose to nose with Desmond. "You're the bestest girl! Yes you are!"

I giggled and knelt beside Jake, putting my arm around his waist and leaning my head on his shoulder. He kissed me, hard. "Thank you. You are also the bestest girl. Also, ow."

"You've got to stop! You promised Sonia." I swatted him on the side. "But thank you, too. Thank you for not giving up on me."

"Awwwwww," Roger squealed from above us, while Desmond, assuming my lovey words were directed at her, nestled her nose into my stomach and pushed until I fell backwards onto my bottom, giggling. Jake scooped me up to kiss me again, and Desmond nosed her way between us til we were all perched in a squishy, furry hug.

"I hate to break up this love fest," Roger said. "But I do need to go."

"Right." I leapt up. Jake joined me with an arm around my waist as Desmond jumped up onto his legs, desperate to be on the same level as everyone else.

"Not me." Jimmy sauntered in from the kitchen, an apple in hand. "I was thinking maybe I'd give Cali a try. I like the vibes here. Could be a new start, don't you think?" He took a bite of the apple, the crisp crunch audible, and wiggled his eyebrows.

"No!" Jake and I said simultaneously.

We took the 10 to the Ontario airport, huge shipping trucks passing us the whole way. I hated the 10, but I did like thinking about the shipping containers—how they'd been in China, filled with goods, and shipped here, how they would go back to China empty—it seemed like such a waste—only to be refilled and sent back again. I wondered if people ever stowed away in the empty containers. Did boats travel faster with them empty? No, it probably had more to do with gulf streams or ocean currents or other things I didn't understand—pretty ironic, given my name. There was so much about the world I didn't know, and for the first time—minus a few brief hours in New York—I felt eager to explore it all.

Thinking of New York reminded me of our current destination, and I moved over to the right lane and drove as slowly as possible to try to extend my time with Roger, who sat beside me in the front seat. In the back, Jake and Jimmy sat on either side with Desmond snuggled in the middle.

"Why are you driving like an old lady?" Roger was never one to mince words.

I sighed. "I don't want to say goodbye."

"You'll be saying goodbye to our friendship if you make me miss my flight."

Behind me, Desmond was licking Jake's nose. Roger was right. The future was inevitable, and clinging to the past wouldn't stop it from arriving. I was ready for the next chapter. I stepped on the gas.

Despite my determination, a knot clenched in my stomach as we approached a sign for the airport exits. Roger was really leaving. I had Jake now, I told myself. I would be okay. But my attempts to reassure myself brought my love for Roger into starker focus. It wasn't about needing him for housing or as my trusty cheerleader. It was about having him around. He'd always been around—since we were kids—and now I would have to figure out how to be an adult without him.

I exited and turned left, away from the foothills and toward large nondescript industrial buildings, built as if they didn't expect to be there long. Airplanes took off and landed.

People parked in lots of convention centers and inns and restaurants. Roger tapped his hands on his crossed legs.

I took a deep breath as I headed toward the departing gates. The layout was confusing, but I managed to find the terminals, even though I'd been hoping getting lost would give me a last few minutes with my friend.

"Terminal One?"

Roger nodded.

There were other cars ahead of us letting people out, and I tried to breathe in the moments.

Soon, it was our turn at the curb.

Jimmy practically rolled from the car. "Stay rude, kids. Thanks for the show."

"Wait," I said. "Did your flying phobia disappear?"

Roger winked. "I gave him a Xanax."

"Probably better than his usual coping mechanisms," Jake muttered.

Jimmy's vociferous response from the curb made it extra clear he had heard the comment. "Most definitely." Now he looked to me. "I think I may even try to score some under my own name. I'm turning a page, friends, turning a page."

And with that, Jimmy Danger strutted toward the airport.

"Dude is weird," Jake said, and Roger agreed, but I smiled as I watched Jimmy go. Weird as he might be, and as implausible as it was, we were connected, and I was glad to see him back on the right track.

Jake tipped his head toward the trunk. "Need help with your stuff, dude?"

"I've got it." Roger got out of the car, and fresh tears pushed at the corners of my eyes as I followed and closed the door behind me.

"Listen." Roger looked at me. "You are going to be fine. Do you hear me? This is exactly how things were supposed to work out."

"I know." I sniffled. "But I'll still miss you."

"Oh, honey, I'll miss you, too. With no one eternally in my debt, I'm going to have to do my own dishes. But you know you can come to New York whenever you want. And you know I won't be able to stay away from my...*our* dog." He tilted his head toward the backseat, and I followed his gesture to where Desmond sat, drooling on Jake's lap. When I returned my gaze to Roger's eyes I saw they were watery, and I remembered his confession the night we'd lit the Hanukkah candles. He was scared, too, and it was my turn to give a pep talk—to be there for my best friend.

"Hey. You're going to be ok."

Roger's facade cracked. "You think?"

"I know. Your family loves you. If they didn't, they wouldn't be trying so hard. And the choir will be lucky to have you. You're an incredible music teacher, and you'll be a role model to so many of those kids."

Roger nodded as a single tear rolled down his cheek.

"Seriously. You're going to fucking kill it. New York better watch out."

Roger grabbed me and we held each other, shaking with silent tears, as I tried to absorb as much of him as I could—to bottle up the feelings of love and safety I had taken for granted for too long.

Finally, I pulled away and wiped my tears with the back of my hand. "Ok, go. Before I really start to cry."

"You think I saved my goodbye with you for last?" Roger teased. He walked over to the back door and opened it. Desmond climbed out of Jake's lap and panted at Roger. Roger bent down and took the dog's face in his hands, whispered something in her ear, and gave her a final scruff. "Jake," Roger said, his arms still around Desmond's neck.

"Yeah?"

"Take care of my girls."

"You know I will."

"And tell your mom thank you. My life would have been a lot darker if she hadn't taken me in."

"I'll tell her," Jake promised.

"Now, go!" Roger stood and turned his attention back to me. "Go home and have fun with your man." I nodded. Roger blew a kiss and headed into the flowing crowd of the airport.

"You okay?" Jake asked when I got back into the car.

"I'll be fine." I meant it. "You don't want to come up to the front?"

Jake looked sheepish as his eyes met mine in the rearview mirror. "I don't want to leave Desmond alone back here."

I laughed. "What did you do before this dog?"

"I honestly don't know."

I exited the airport. When I got back onto the freeway, I took my time and looked around as I drove, taking in the shops and roads that had always been home. It would feel empty without Roger, I knew, but there was already a new kind of fullness too.

From the backseat, Jake talked about all the things we would do together—the shows we would go to, the dinner parties we would have—could I imagine Romero in a suit?—and finally...our moms.

"Should we call them?" I asked. They would be so happy Jake and I were together.

Jake laughed. "I almost don't want to give them the satisfaction."

"I know!"

"But yeah, who's first?"

"Call yours," I said.

But as it turned out, it didn't matter who we called first, because when Jake dialed Mrs. Rosenblatt's number and put the call on speaker, she picked up and began talking immediately. "You won't believe who I'm with! So I ran into Rainbow Grimspoon again at Stater Bros. There was a sale on kale this time, but you know I never know what to do with kale. I always buy it and then it sits in the crisper until it goes limp, and you know how I hate cleaning wilted leaves out of the crisper. So I was standing in front of the kale, going back and forth—should I buy it? Should I leave it?"

"So I gave her my recipe for baked kale chips." My heart stopped as I recognized Rainbow's voice.

"And we started talking," Mrs. Rosenblatt went on. "And we realized you two were off together doing your little show."

"Why didn't you tell me you were doing a show?" Rainbow asked, but before I could answer, Mrs. Rosenblatt continued.

"I think I would prefer not knowing to knowing and not being invited. Anyway, we decided if our children are having a good time, why can't we go do something fun? You know mothering is a full-time job, even when your kids are grown. I always thought when you were out of the house, I would stop worrying about you, but no. No one tells you it's a lifetime commitment—the worrying."

"So, we're at my house," Rainbow said. "I have buckwheat pancakes on the stove and kale chips in the oven." The image of Mrs. Rosenblatt at Rainbow's made my heart skip a beat. Did she know what marijuana smelled like? When was the last time Mariska had cleaned?

"And Rainbow is going to show me how she celebrates Hanukkah. It sounds quite unique. Traditions are important, of course, but so is change. Flexibility! The Torah says we need to determine when to be steadfast and when to be flexible, and Rainbow has helped me realize I've been stuck in my ways for too long. Although, it *is* possible to be too flexible. Do you remember when Mrs. Sheffield decided to explore Kabbalah?"

"Kabbalah is a fascinating subject," Rainbow cut in. "It speaks to the mystic origins of most modern religions. We forget sometimes how magical the events in the old texts really were."

"All well and good," Mrs. Rosenblatt said. "But Judy shaved her head and left her family for a ten-month meditation retreat in the Catskills. As if spending her children's college fund signified such spiritual growth."

As our mothers continued to talk, and Jake and I continued toward home, we exchanged gawking glances, both our mouths ajar.

"Wow," Jake said, when there was finally a break in their discussion. "This...is an interesting development."

"Is your mother not allowed her own friends, Jakey? You know, people don't grow out of the need for friendship. I don't need you to judge—"

"No," Jake interrupted. "I think it's great. We uh...we have something to tell you two, too."

"What did I say?" Mrs. Rosenblatt asked, and I could picture her throwing her hands in the air—a gesture of exasperated correctness. "I always knew you two would find your way back to each other. A mother knows."

"It was in the cards," Rainbow agreed. Then, after a pause: "I have good news, too."

"What is it?" I asked.

"There's an artists' community in Poland I've been in touch with for several years. The owner is an old lover of mine."

"Rainbow. TMI." I clicked on the turn signal and took the exit toward my house. Our house. I could still hardly believe it. But wait—an artists' community? Poland?

"Anyway, I think it's finally time. I think you're ready," Rainbow said.

Wait, what? She thought *I* was ready? All this time...had Rainbow thought she was taking care of me?

"The toilet was a wakeup call. I need to be more self-sufficient. And I need to let you live your life, too. I'm a capable woman when I decide to be, and I need to let you discover your purpose...without worrying about me."

I shook my head, unsure what to make of this news.

"I'm just sad she'll be going right as we reconnected," Mrs. Rosenblatt said. "Lonely again."

"Don't worry, mom. Sailor and I will come visit all the time."

I was still in shock, the colors of the world extra vivid, but I smiled at Jake to assure him I was happy to do mom social calls.

"And my residency is only ten weeks," Rainbow said. I'd been worried about finding someone to watch the house—and I'd decided I was done burdening you. But then Elaine told me she'd been planning to downsize—"

"Downsize?" Jake asked. "Is this why you wanted me to go through my stuff?"

"Yes, Jakey. You know I'm not required to be your free storage unit."

"So I told her she can move into your old room, Sailor."

"Obviously we'll have to do a little renovating," Mrs. Rosenblatt cut in. "But with the money from my house....You know I could use a change, Jakey. I've been stagnant for too long."

Jake nodded enthusiastically, eyes wide.

"Well, we'd better get back to our pancakes and kale," Mrs. Rosenblatt said.

"Yes," Rainbow said. "We have so much to plan before I go."

"Enjoy your pancakes?" I was still processing everything they had told us. "And...kale?" Jake hung up.

"Wow," he said. "That...was not on my BINGO card."

I laughed. "Mine neither. But apparently we were on theirs."

"They must be having a ball dissecting this right now. They're probably planning our wedding."

I laughed again as I tried to ignore the tiny flutter Jake's words had caused in my chest. I had never been one to imagine my nuptials, but with Jake...maybe. "Wait til we tell them about their grand-dog."

I couldn't ignore the ideas already rolling through my brain—Roger would be my best man, of course, Desmond could be Jake's maid of honor. Would the band be up for another reunion? Were things with Hillary ok enough to ask her to do vocals?

I took a deep breath and reminded myself to stay in the moment. I had been looking outside myself for so long, telling myself all I had was music, or drums, or Roger. I'd thrown myself wholeheartedly into ska or friendship or dog ownership, thinking obsession would save me. I wouldn't make that mistake with Jake again. I could have all of those things—music, Desmond, Roger, Jake—but I wouldn't let any of them be the entire basis of my identity. If I had learned anything over the past week, it was that all I really had—all any of us really have—is this moment—and right now, this moment was perfect.

We arrived at the house. I turned the car key and listened to the engine sputter off, then opened the car door and stepped out into the crisp Southern California winter. Already, I could feel Roger's absence, and I had to remind myself he was a phone call away. Together, the three of us—Jake, Desmond, and I, walked inside. We were home. It was the last night of Hanukkah, and we had no candles of our own to light, but it didn't matter. I had never felt further from the dark.

EPILOGUE

"**A**re we really going to this Purim spiel?" Jake asked. Desmond sat at his feet wearing a dog hoodie and dog visor. Her dog sunglasses lay on the shoe bench by the door waiting for their next walk. Almost three months had passed since the Barn reunion show, and Desmond was thriving. The dog rarely left Jake's side, and neither of them would have it any other way.

Jake and I, too, were happier than we could have imagined. "Yes!" I said. "It's classic rock themed, and you know your mom really wants to go." I'd been going to lots of synagogue functions with Mrs. Rosenblatt—everything from Sisterhood book clubs to fundraisers to Torah study. Our new band—me, Jake, Sonia, Go, and Romero, had even been invited to play for the Temple's casino night thanks to Jake's brilliant idea to incorporate Klezmer influences. On most Fridays, Jake and the moms and I celebrated Shabbat together by lighting beeswax candles at Rainbow and Mrs. Rosenblatt's place, which had, indeed, begun to transform from a hippie haven into something of a happy medium—tidy and organized, but still decorated in Rainbow's eccentric fashion.

"You're not worried the music will be too mainstream?" Jake teased, though he didn't sound surprised. In the past couple months, I'd broadened my musical taste, branching out into indie, hip hop, and yes, classic rock. He had even convinced me to indulge in a little country now and then—a guilty pleasure he had inherited from Hillary.

"I mean, I can get down to some Rolling Stones."

Jake laughed as I sat across from him at the kitchen table and bent to pull up my checkered tights.

"Oh, shit!" He wiggled his eyebrows. "It's a tights day! So that means…?"

"Yup. You'll have to control your boner at Temple."

"Dammit!"

Between us sat a hand painted pot Rainbow had sent during her time in Poland. In it grew a thriving succulent my mother had propagated from one of her neighborhood burglaries. Someone had finally complained. Mrs. Rosenblatt had told us the story of Mr. Espinoza—how he had knocked on the door and said he'd noticed they had all the same varieties, and several of his plants had shown signs of fungal infection after leaves had been improperly removed. Mrs. Rosenblatt had apologized and moved all of Rainbow's plant children to the back yard, aside from this one, which she'd given to Jake and me as a housewarming gift when Jake moved in.

"How was work?" Jake asked.

"It was fun. You should see this sixth grader. She's so into the percussion instruments. I practically had to wrestle the glockenspiel away from her."

Jake laughed.

"I had to promise her I'd buy the whole class shaky eggs for the holidays. Teachers' salaries suck, but I could never have afforded it with my freelance money. I really should thank Hillary again for backing up Roger's recommendation."

"Don't give her too much credit. You know she was worried they'd cut the music department budget more if they didn't find a good replacement for both her and Roger. All her prayers would have been in vain."

"She was being nice," I said. "I think it was genuine altruism. And besides, she's happy with her new fiancé."

In the 80ish days since she'd shown up at The Barn, Hillary had gotten engaged to the man from her parents' church. All her social media updates this week had included "#blessed."

I knew Jake only refrained from making a snarky comment about this now because of the private message Hillary had sent the night before.

The Decklands had banned Jake from the wedding, she'd told him, but when Hillary's niece Sofie had protested, they'd caved and said both of us could attend the rehearsal dinner. Jake was less than thrilled about interacting with Alan Deckland again, but he was so cute when he talked about introducing me to Sofie.

"You've turned into a softy," Jake told me now, and I had to admit a few months of therapy had chilled me out a good deal. I still thought most of my happier demeanor was thanks to taking over Roger's gig as a music teacher. Rather than dulling my edges, it seemed to have sharpened them, like I was even more myself. I felt guilty for enjoying it so much sometimes. Jake's own job was still boring, but he had made peace with the daily drudgery. Sometimes, work was just work and there wasn't much to do about it, he said. Besides, with our salaries combined, we would eventually have money for cool projects. Once we'd paid off Jake's dental bills and replenished the savings we'd depleted with the New York trip, we were planning to xeriscape the lawn. Someday, we wanted to backpack Europe and visit the cities in Poland and Czechia where our ancestors had lived.

"Speaking of softies, I heard from Roger today," I said.

"Yeah?"

"Yeah...he has a boyfriend. And guess what—he's Jewish!"

"I could have guessed, in fact."

"Not just the boyfriend. Roger is too. He converted! He's officially part of our tribe."

"Finally!"

Jake's phone rang, and he looked down at the screen. "Speaking of New York, this is a New York area code. Who's this?"

I glanced at the screen and shrugged. "Not Roger." I slipped my feet into my chunky Mary Janes.

Jake answered and put the call on speaker as he continued to button his shirt. "Hello?"

"Hey...Jake. It's Jerome Higgins."

Across the table, my eyebrows shot up.

"Jerome!" Jake said, pausing with his fingers on a button.

"So, I wanted to talk to you..." Jerome's voice was slightly staticky as Jake and I looked at one another. "I'm starting a camp out in LA."

I could practically hear Jake's heart start beating like a snare drum in his chest. My own echoed it as we waited, eyes locked.

"I need someone on the ground there to manage the legal side of things."

Jake didn't let him finish. "Yeah....yes...absolutely!" Beside him, I whisper screamed. "Thank you. Yes. Thank you for the opportunity. I'm honored."

"Can we talk logistics? Or I can call back later."

Jake looked to me, and I nodded permission. "No. Now is good. I have a few minutes."

It was hard to focus on Jerome's words as he went into detail about the organization and how he envisioned Jake's new role, but I gleaned enough to absorb the basics.

He would be putting his degree to work—there was no way his mom could object—but he'd be doing it for an organization he cared about—one that made a differ ence, and where he could work alongside other cool people. Jerome wanted him to start immediately.

As Higgins went on, I stood, shaking with adrenaline, and went back to our bedroom to grab a pair of earrings. I could't wait to see Mrs. Rosenblatt's reaction to the news. After slipping the delicate black posts into my piercings, I paused and looked at myself in the mirror, trying to fully absorb what was happening in the other room, and smiled at my reflection. If I was a different person, I'd be posting "#blessed" myself.

"I know this is a lot," Jerome was saying as I retook my seat across from Jake. "Don't worry if you didn't catch it all—I'm available any time."

Jake exhaled, and after more effusive thanks and a plan to talk again on Monday, ended the call.

I jumped up. "Jake! This is incredible!" I hugged him, then pulled back. "I was worried for a minute something had happened to Jimmy Danger."

"Me too. For some reason, I carry a strange fondness for the man who helped bring me back to you. But I have another reason to like him now, too."

"Yeah?"

"Yup. He recommended me. Jerome saw the videos of our show online and used them as an excuse to reach out to Jimmy. He's in rehab, apparently. Made amends with Tony and everything. The three of them caught up and are even talking about doing an acoustic album together."

My smile grew wider. "Ahhh, I'm so glad! And who would have thought Jimmy Danger would make a good job reference?"

"Right? But yeah. Me too. I'm glad he's getting it together." I knew Jake meant it. Jimmy deserved a happy ending, too.

My grin grew mischievous. "But acoustic? What sellouts."

Jake laughed. "I saw Nirvana Unplugged on your playlist last week."

I put my hands up, feigning ignorance. "I have no idea how that got there."

"I almost forgot the best part." Jake was trying and failing to contain his ear to ear smile. "Jerome said he'll need me in New York four times a year for quarterly check ins—all expenses paid."

He watched me with a grin as the implications sunk in. When they did a moment later, I squealed. "We'll get to go see Roger!"

Jake beamed. "Yup!"

"Do you know the dates yet? We should let Sonia know so we can reschedule practices. I know she has to request evenings off pretty far ahead of time, and I'll have to get time off too—see if a sub can cover my classes."

"I'll ask Monday." Jake grinned. "Hey…"

"Hm?"

"We have a little time before we need to leave for Temple. Do you want to listen to *Happy Skalidays*?"

"It's March," I said. "Even Rainbow has taken down her Winter Solstice Tree."

"Do you care?"

"No."

We laughed.

Jake found the album amidst our collection and carefully ripped into the plastic, then slid the record from its sleeve. The vinyl was perfect—striped red and white like a candy cane, its grooves clean and deep. He carried the record to our turntable—a vintage 1970s set rescued from Mrs. Rosenblatt's attic during her downsizing. It fit our new decor perfectly. We'd worked hard to make the house feel like it belonged to both of us—from the checkerboard backsplash we'd installed in the kitchen to the flyer from the reunion show, which we'd had professionally framed. It was a perfect blend of grown-up and ska.

Jake flipped the turntable on and watched as the vinyl started to spin, then carefully set the needle into its grooves. We stood still and waited for the first track to play.

It was better on vinyl, like music always was. The Internet had not done this album justice. On vinyl, the horns felt like they were close—I could imagine they were in the room with us. Jimmy Danger's voice was clear with raw emotion, and I could almost believe we'd been transported back ten years—that listening to the album was a kind of magic—that it captured time and made that show eternal. But it was the same kind of magic music always enacted, I thought, as I let it work its splendor on me and the man I loved. Looking at Jake, I knew he felt it too. Some things didn't need magic to stay true.

Acknowledgements (Skank-yous)

Thank you first and most to my husband Jer, for all of his support for this book and for me. I love you. I hope everything I write for the rest of my life reflects it. Thank you, Eric, for the conversation that planted the idea for this book and for the promotional graphics. Thank you to MU330 for their album *Winter Wonderland*, which I have listened to every holiday season since I was seventeen. Thank you, Jen DeLuca, for picking me for #KissPitch and being such an amazing mentor. To my fellow #KissPitch writers, thank you for all the support and encouragement during the process of revision, submission, and publishing. I am so proud of all of you. Thank you to Josephine and Madeline at Covers and Cupcakes for the beautiful cover. And to my family, friends, former teachers, and other readers, thank you for reading and sharing my work. I appreciate every one of you.

About the Ska-thor

Becca Spence Dobias grew up in West Virginia, where she was also a weird Jewish ska-punk kid. She now lives in Southern California with her husband and two children. *Pick It Up!* is her second novel. Her first, *On Home,* came out in 2021.